Summer
Entanglements

Book 1 in The Guesthouse Girls Series

Judy Ann Koglin

Maui Shores Publishing

Kihei 2020

D0745777

Summer Entanglements Copyright © 2020
by Maui Shores Publishing

Kihei, HI 96753
www.mauishorespublishing.com

Unless otherwise indicated, Scripture quotations are from:
The Holy Bible, American Standard Version (ASV)

Library of Congress Control Number:2020918897

ISBN 978-1-953799-00-5 (pbk)
ISBN 978-1-953799-01-2 (e-book)

Acknowledgements

Writing a book was a new process for me and there was a learning curve to climb. This journey was made easier with help from many people.

I extend grateful thanks to my faithful proofreading staff of Kay Koglin, Kathy Koglin, Nola Schulenburg, and Jo Sorrell. Each of you helped immensely.

Also, many thanks to my clever and diplomatic editor Savannah Cottrell who helped me flesh out sections that lacked detail and helped elevate this book to a level worthy of publication.

I so appreciate the efforts of my beautiful and talented cover designer, Joanna Alonzo, who designed a cover to precisely capture my vision.

Lastly, I acknowledge my husband who patiently listened to me during our nightly walks as I inundated him with updates about the daily adventures in the lives of The Guesthouse Girls. Thank you for indulging me in this endeavor, as writing one book catapulted into seven, with more in the works! Your wisdom and encouragement were exactly what I needed!

The ideas for the characters and story lines represented in this book were a blessing from God and my hope is that Summer Entanglements will, yes--be enjoyable and entertaining--but ultimately, make a difference in someone's life. I leave the results to Him.

Major Characters

Amie Larson – this tiny blonde Chelan native works at her family's Lakeshore Resort and is positive and encouraging.

Emma Martinez – has long dark perfect curls and eyes that gleam with enthusiasm. She is from Pasco but is working at Femley's General Store in Chelan this summer.

Hope Stevens – an introverted three-sport athlete from Lynnwood who is working at her uncle's boat rental business to earn money for college.

Kendi Arnold – an artistic redhead who loves to play instruments and sing. She is working her dream summer job at Brandon's Coffee and Bakeshop.

Aunty Nola Milton – this 70-year-old lady is the owner of The Guesthouse and hosts four teenage girls each summer. She is fashionable and kind. She loves hosting the girls because it keeps her young.

Ben Brandon – a friendly blond seventeen-year-old barista works for his parents at Brandon's Coffee and Bakeshop.

Ryan Sanders – This brown-haired senior at Chelan High is the assistant manager of the Slip and Slide waterpark. He is flirtatious and has a smile that melts the hearts of girls from all over the Northwest.

CHAPTER ONE
Leaving Home

"Don't forget to warn the Olsens about the ceiling fan in the family room, make sure they have Mom's phone number and mine and Uncle Bob's in case they have any problems, and ..."

"Dad," Amie implored, "Stop. We've been over this 50 times, and the list hasn't changed."

"Make sure you take your vitamins and be a big help at the resort," her mom cut in, "Call us and tell us how everything is going and let us know when you've settled in at the guesthouse."

"Yes, mom," Amie sighed with a slight edge in her voice that was a combination of annoyance and amusement. "I'll be fine, the Olsens will be fine, the house will be fine, and you guys will be fine taking care of Grandpa Peterson in Montana. You already moved my stuff to Aunty Nola's for me, and we know almost every person in Chelan, so I have plenty of people looking out for me. Stop worrying about me and get going! Have a great summer…and I love you. I will text you, but I can't until you leave!"

1

Amie Larson and her mom looked very similar with their petite figures, pale blonde hair, and blue eyes. Amie's mom was a clipboard person, always making sure tasks were taken care of, even more so now that she and her husband were leaving Chelan for the whole summer. Amie was more relaxed in her approach, even though she did a great job with her responsibilities. One trait they did share was their love of fashion and shopping and, even though her mom always had a well-organized plan while shopping and Amie preferred to browse leisurely, they still loved to shop together.

Amie laughed as she hugged her parents and waved as they drove out of sight. She adjusted the collar on her red and white nautical summer romper and thought, *Okay, Amie, you're on your own.* This thought would have been very scary if she was truly on her own, but her parents made sure she would be well taken care of this summer.

Amie hopped on her bike and rode the quarter mile between her family's large lakeside home and the Lakeshore Resort in the middle of town. Many years ago, when Great-Grandpa Larson first bought the property, the Lakeshore Resort was just a small rustic motel by the lake. He eventually expanded it, as did his son, Amie's Grandpa Larson, when he eventually took it over. Now, the third generation managed the expanded property. Amie's Uncle Bob and his highly capable wife Debbie functioned well together as co-general managers of the popular Lakeshore Resort.

Amie's mom Staci was the resort's accountant, and Amie's dad Randy oversaw maintenance for the entire property. This summer, Staci would be doing the accounting remotely from Montana. With the major maintenance projects already taken care of in the off season, Amie's dad felt comfortable leaving his long-time assistant in charge for the summer. Randy had assured his crew that he was only a six-hour drive away in Missoula if there was any sort of urgent matter that he needed to come back for. The money Amie's parents would earn from renting their lake house for 14 weeks would be about enough to fund Amie's first year of college, depending on the school she chose.

Amie parked her bike and sat down at Beaches, the lunch counter restaurant at the resort and ordered a cheeseburger and Sprite from Josh, a blond boy who'd just recently graduated from Chelan High where she would be a junior in the fall.

When he brought out her lunch, he gave her a big smile that showed off his perfectly white teeth and said, "Hey Amie, I heard you were going to be working here at the resort this summer. That's cool! What'll you be doing?"

"Anything they tell me to do, I guess." Amie shrugged with a grin, biting into her juicy cheeseburger. *Was it her imagination, or had Josh become super cute lately?* She took a second look at him. He was about five foot ten and muscular with light blue eyes and Scandinavian good-looks. He was already sporting a tan and he looked like he could be her brother, if she had one.

Well, there was no time to consider that, because just then, she felt the buzz of a text in her pocket, letting her know that the Olsen family had arrived and were ready to be checked into her house for the summer.

Amie finished her burger and looked around to say goodbye to Josh, but he was busy helping another customer. She went out to where she had left her bike and rode the short distance back to her family's home. Along the way, she caught glimpses of the majestic lake to her left and the evergreen trees on the hills to the right. She enjoyed the warmth of the late spring sun on her back. She smelled the sweet fragrance of wildflowers in the fresh air and felt like she must be one of the most fortunate girls in the world to live year-round in a place that tourists spent thousands of dollars to visit for a week. She looked forward to the lake warming up a bit more so she could go swimming and water skiing without a wetsuit. Amie waved as one of her neighbors passed by in their car and marveled at the near-empty road she was riding on. She knew that in a week or two, this road would be so crowded with carloads of tourists that it would be impossible to ride her bike on it, so she relished every second.

She met the Olsen family at her house and showed them around and explained a quirk with one of the ceiling fans. She then gave them the remote control for the garage, the keys to the house and the pool gate, and the list of important contact phone numbers. When the Olsens had all their questions answered, Amie left them alone to enjoy their accommodations.

As she rode her bike back to town, she felt very grown up because, although she had helped out at the resort in many capacities over the last few years, this was the first year she would officially be on summer staff–with a time card and paycheck and everything! She would even be living on her own for the very first time, too...well, maybe not *exactly* on her own, but a big step toward being independent.

This might just be the best summer ever!

◊ ◊◊◊ ◊

Emma Martinez felt the pressure of her fingertips nervously rapping on the console between the two back seats in her parents' car. She rearranged her long, dark curls behind her white headband for the tenth time. "How much longer until we get there?"

"Still another hour, Mija," her mom replied. "Remember, it is a three-hour drive from Pasco."

Emma had tried to convince her parents to stop calling her the slang term for "my daughter" in public because she didn't always want to draw attention to the obvious fact that she hailed from another culture. However, Emma did enjoy that her mom still called her "Mija" when only the family was around. Emma knew that she was going to miss her sweet, intelligent mom and her goofy dad this summer, and she probably would even have a moment or two when she missed her little sister Riley. The girls were several years apart but had shared a lot of secrets and laughter throughout the years.

Emma was excited to meet the three girls who would also be staying at The Guesthouse this summer. Aunty Nola, as Mrs. Milton was affectionately called, hosted summer workers who came to help fill the dozens of summer jobs that opened up due to the huge influx of vacationers to the resort town of Chelan. During Emma's interview for Femley's General Store, Mr. Femley told her that the population more than doubled between Memorial Day and Labor Day. He said that sometimes, the store would have lines out the door for those who wanted to buy anything from sunscreen and inflatable water toys to Femley's specialty ice cream.

"We can hardly keep up with the demand!" Mr. Femley had exclaimed while she sat there in his office. Emma was slightly taken aback by his enthusiasm, but at the same time, it was reassuring somehow. "Our customers will keep us on our toes all summer, but we are grateful for all the visitors because all the business they give us keeps us going during the slower wintertime."

This spring, after Mr. Femley called Emma to offer her the position, Mrs. Martinez took the phone to ask Mr. Femley about housing suggestions. Mr. Femley had referred her to Aunty Nola's Guesthouse and gave her the contact information. "If you want your daughter to be in a safe environment with someone who will love her like she is her own, you need to check out this place. Aunty Nola is the best," Mr. Femley advised her mom.

Emma applied to The Guesthouse and was thrilled when she was chosen for one of the rooms this summer.

Emma felt her heart pound a little thinking of starting her first real job Monday. She couldn't wait to greet customers and help them find just what they needed. She had been a member of Future Business Leaders of America during the school year and knew that this would be a summer filled with the real-world job experiences that she wanted, perfect for scholarships and a future resume far down the line. Emma was passionate about small business and had huge admiration for entrepreneurs who had figured out how to weather the storms of business ownership. She hoped that this summer, she would be able to conduct some interviews with business owners and compile them for inclusion in a blog she was going to start with her club in the fall.

"I wonder if your roommates will be nice." Eleven year-old Riley broke the silence with a gleam in her dark brown eyes. "They could be the best friends you've ever met...or they could be a nightmare and steal your stuff and play loud music when you want to sleep and make you wish you had never come to Chelan."

"Quit trying to scare her, Riley," their dad glanced back briefly before returning his gaze to the road. "Mrs. Milton carefully screens and checks references of all the young ladies who stay at her guest house so we can be confident that Emma's roommates will be nice girls. Remember, Aunty Nola had a long talk with both mom and me when she interviewed Emma. Now, if all you ladies are finished talking let's get back to listening to this podcast. This is supposed to be his best show yet."

7

And with that, Emma's dad pushed the radio's volume button, and the last hour of the trip passed very quickly as the comedian told hilarious stories one right after another.

◊ ◊◊◊ ◊

Kendi Arnold smoothed her reddish-brown hair wistfully as she looked in the mirror with her best friend – her "BFF" as she called her – Bella. "I wonder how my hair will look in a hairnet all summer as I sell pastries and coffee."

"Who cares? You are going to be in Chelan–it's only the top resort town in the whole state!" Bella exclaimed proudly. "I am so jealous, and I can't wait to visit you if your housemother will let me!"

"I'll check out the scene when I get there and text you," Kendi's green eyes sparkled.

"Of course I will need to check out the cute tourist boys with you. I can't let you have them all to yourself! There definitely aren't any cute boys here to check out!" Bella whined as Kendi nodded. Kendi was not nearly as interested in boys as Bella was; her thoughts were more consumed with excitement about her new job than they were with relationships with boys.

"I hope you won't like your roommates more than me," Bella said, twirling one of her blonde curls.

"Oh, you know that nobody can replace you!"

"Ok…well, I'd better get going so you and your parents can get on the road. Text me every time something newsworthy happens!"

"You know I will, and you better do the same!" The girls hugged and took a selfie so Bella could post it. They said a tearful goodbye, and Bella headed home. Kendi and Bella had been best friends since they met in first grade when Bella first moved to Kendi's neighborhood in Redmond, Washington. Kendi heard there was a girl her age moving into the house down the street and she and her mom baked cookies and brought them over to share with the new family. Bella came to the door and grabbed Kendi's hand and led her to her bedroom and the two little girls played with Bella's dolls and stuffed animals while their mom's drank coffee. By the time her mom was ready to leave, Kendi and Bella had already created a special handshake and vowed to play together whenever their moms would let them. As the girls had grown older, their interests went in different directions. Bella became more interested in boys, teen magazines, and social media; and Kendi developed her skills in playing the piano and the guitar and worked really hard at earning her straight A average. Despite their growing differences, the girls remained close friends and enjoyed spending time together whenever they had the chance.

A few minutes later, Kendi's dad came into the room cautiously. "Is it safe to come in? Has the Wonder Twins' power deactivated?"

"Dad...you know that phrase is outdated. I still don't even know what it means." She rolled her eyes and gave a sigh. "Anyway, are you guys about ready to go?

I can't believe that my first shift starts at 6 o'clock on Monday! 6 a.m. for a teenager is cruel and unusual."

"You won't say that at 2:30 in the afternoon when you are off work and headed to the lake!" Kendi's mom remarked as she came into the room and put her arm around her daughter's shoulders. "Let's get moving, little girl. We have a three-hour drive ahead of us."

"More than that when we have to stop at every Starbucks," her dad Phil said with feigned exasperation.

They got in the minivan and headed out. Kendi's mom peppered her with questions about the job and the living situation, even though she already knew most of the answers.

Kendi decided to ask because she knew her mom was just feeling nostalgic: "Mom, where did you work when you lived in Chelan?"

"Well, one summer I worked at the record store, and the other summer I worked at the video store—neither of which exist anymore, of course."

"A sign of the times. Who could have predicted that?" Kendi's dad marveled." The vast changes in technology since then are really amazing when you think about it."

"Well," Kendi commented, "I don't think that a bakery and coffee shop will ever be replaced by technology. Maybe my own daughter will work there someday."

"Maybe so," her mom laughed. "One thing I do know is that Chelan is a magical place to spend the summer, and I know you will make many great memories."

◊ ◊◊◊ ◊

Yes! Another personal best! Hope Stevens thought to herself as she practically fell through the door and peeled her headphones off, her long dark blond ponytail damp with sweat from her run. She recorded her time in a log on her phone. *Next year's soccer season will be epic if I can continue to run and keep in shape while I'm in Chelan.*

She headed to the shower, then dressed and surveyed the contents of her suitcase. Hope always tended to pack lightly. She wasn't like some of the other girls she knew who had closets bursting with more clothes and shoes than they could ever need. She was proud of being a minimalist and even felt a little sense of pride that her passion was sports and fitness and not shopping and giggling with the girls about the hot guys at school.

Hope Stevens was on a mission, and she was not about to let unimportant things get in the way. That's why when her mom's brother Joe called and asked if she could come and help rent jet skis to tourists, Hope jumped at the chance. Frankly, she could stand to have a change of pace, and her mom might enjoy having their small apartment to herself this summer. Her mom was always stressed and had to work two jobs to make ends meet to and try to save for Hope's college tuition.

Hope was thankful that her mom wanted her to have a better life than she had as a teenager and was grateful that her mom sacrificed so much for her, but now that she was almost 16, Hope wanted to do her part.

When Hope's mom Megan found out she was pregnant when she was sixteen–a child herself– she chose to keep her baby, even when a lot of pregnant teenage girls were making different choices back then. She worked hard to make the best life possible for the two of them.

Hope looked at the meager contents of her duffel bag again, shrugged, and added another pair of shorts and t-shirt, zipping up the bag quickly. She texted her mom, knowing that Megan wouldn't see the text until her half-hour lunch period at noon: *"Headed to the bus now. Don't worry about me this summer. I'll be fine working with Uncle Joe. Love you, Mom!"*

◊ ◊◊◊ ◊

Amie knocked on the door of the Guesthouse and was greeted with a hug from Aunty Nola. As a lifelong resident of the small town of Chelan, Amie knew almost all the longtime residents.

Aunty Nola was an attractive 70-year-old lady who lived in the same large farmhouse that she grew up in. She met her husband Garry when she was in her senior year of high school when he had come to town to work as a laborer in Nola's parent's expansive apple orchard. It was love at first sight for Nola, but it took about a year for Garry to ask her out. Once they had their first date, it didn't take long for them to realize that they were meant to be, and they were married in a small but beautiful ceremony at the local Baptist church later that year.

Garry continued to work for Nola's parents, and the couple eventually took over the management of the orchard after her parents retired. During that time, they had success and diligently saved their money.

When Garry passed away twelve years ago, Nola hired someone else to run the orchard. She renovated the big farmhouse into a beautiful guesthouse that she used to house four students every summer when they came to help fill all the jobs that were needed during the busy summer tourist season. During the rest of the year, she rented rooms to skiers when they came to spend a week hitting the slopes at the nearby resort.

As she explained to reporter Yvonne Getzen of the *Chelan Gazette* one time, "Renting rooms to summer employees at very affordable rates when other lodging rates are prohibitively high is my way of giving back to the town that had been so good to me."

"Hi Amie, welcome to your new home!" Aunty Nola greeted her warmly as she released their embrace. "Did your parents' renters get settled in your house? How does it feel to have them there?"

"Yes, they seem like a very nice family," Amie told her. "It will be weird knowing someone else is living in our house, and there will be a five-year-old girl living in my room, but I know they'll really enjoy the summer there."

"And you will have a lot of fun here too, Amie!" Aunty Nola assured her. "I am so glad you applied for one of the rooms. It will be fun to spend time with you this summer."

13

"It worked out really great since my parents had to leave town to take care of Grandpa. They can make some money renting our house during high season, and I get to stay in town and work at the resort. Thank you so much for letting me rent one of your rooms, Aunty," Amie said with another hug. "By the way, when do the other girls arrive?"

Aunty Nola consulted her notebook. "Kendi and Emma and their parents should be here in the next hour, and I will pick Hope up at the bus station at 5:00 tonight. You'll be available for the welcome dinner, right?"

"Wouldn't miss it! I think I'll go decorate my room now because I know I'll be really busy at the resort starting tomorrow."

With that, Amie literally danced up the stairs and set her sights upon organizing her room with the ten suitcases that she and her parents had moved in yesterday. Ten suitcases were a bit much to bring to The Guesthouse, but since other people would be occupying her room at her own house this summer, she decided to bring everything rather than putting some of it into the storage unit that her parents had rented. She spread her pretty new blue and white striped comforter on the twin bed that was provided with the room.

The next hour flew by and, as she was putting the final touches on her room, she heard Aunty Nola call out excitedly, "Hey Amie, do you want to come down? I see a car arriving, it is probably one of our new roommates!"

Amie felt a little skip in her heart. She was so excited to meet the other girls who would be staying in The Guesthouse this summer, but she also felt apprehensive about whether they would all get along.

Excitement and curiosity won the battle, and she raced down the sturdy oak stairs and caught a glimpse of a short girl with dark curly hair, her mom, her dad, and a younger girl who looked like she might be a younger sister making their way toward the front deck with Emma's luggage and other items in tow.

◊ ◊◊◊ ◊

Emma's little sister Riley scurried to the door first clutching Emma's brown and white stuffed dog.

Aunty Nola flung open the door with a big smile. "You must be Riley! Emma told me about you when we talked before." She next greeted Hank and Lina, Emma's mom and dad, and then turned her attention to Emma, who hung back a little. Aunty Nola greeted her with a hug and drew all of them into the living room and introduced them to Amie, who had come into the room with a welcoming smile on her face. The girls sized each other up, and Amie was relieved to see that Emma looked like she would be really nice.

"I love your outfit," Emma exclaimed, eying Amie's red and white striped romper. It looks perfect for summer!"

"Thank you," Amie replied. "I like your outfit too. It looks like we are about the same size. There may be some fun clothing and sandal swaps happening in the near future!"

"Sounds good to me!" Emma agreed. Riley took Emma's hand and gave it a tug.

"I want to see your room, Emma!"

"So you shall, my dear," Aunty Nola motioned toward the stairs, "Let's all head up there. I reserved the room next to Amie for you. The two of you will share a bathroom, but it is large."

All four of the guest rooms were identical, and each pair shared a spacious jack-and-jill bathroom.

Sometime during the tour, little Riley heard a car pull up, and she ran downstairs. "Someone else is here!" she yelled up the stairs enthusiastically. Riley's dark curls, so similar to Emma's, bounced as she raced to the window.

"That must be Kendi," Aunty Nola explained as she hurried toward the stairs followed by the rest of the group.

Kendi and her parents arrived at the front door and were welcomed by Aunty Nola as well as Emma, Emma's parents and sister, and Amie. "This is Phil and Beth Arnold and their daughter Kendi," Nola introduced warmly.

After exchanging pleasantries with Kendi and her parents, Emma's dad mentioned that they'd better get back on the road so they could get back home before it got dark. Emma slowly walked her family to their car. The sisters hugged each other and held back tears. "First Joey goes to the army and now you're leaving for the summer. I guess I get mom and dad to myself," Riley stated, not sure whether to be happy or sad.

Emma's mom assured both girls that the time would pass quickly, and they would see her again the first week of July when they came for their annual visit at their timeshare.

"You better plan on buying stuff from me at Mr. Femley's store every day when you come," Emma challenged.

"Oh, the hardships I must go through for the love of my daughter," her mom teased.

"I'll start saving my money now," Emma's dad laughed as he pulled her into a hug, "Now let's get on the road! Love ya kid!"

With many assurances that they would call and text each other, the Martinez family drove off, leaving part of their hearts behind at Aunty Nola's Guesthouse.

With the Martinez family on their way home, Aunty Nola turned her attention to Kendi's family.

They also took a tour of The Guesthouse and helped set up Kendi's room as they got to know Amie. Kendi's mom Beth shared Amie's love of fashion, so they discussed their favorite places to shop and the best times to visit Nordstrom for good deals. Emma soon joined them, and the girls chatted excitedly about themselves and the summer jobs they would soon be starting.

Kendi was excited to try her hand at being a barista, even though the early hours seemed in direct opposition to her natural bent. She loved creating new coffee drinks at home for her family, and she hoped she could bring some of her creativity to the coffee house.

The manager Mark had warned her in advance over the phone after she'd successfully completed her interview and gotten the job that she would probably be selling pastries a lot of the time, but she would be trained on the espresso counter as well. Kendi loved to sing and play the guitar and keyboard and hoped she would have a chance to perform once or twice this summer when they had live music.

Kendi was no stranger to Chelan. She and her family had visited many times in the past, both during the summer and on winter ski trips. It was definitely a family favorite vacation spot, and her parents always kicked around the possibility of purchasing some land nearby so they could come more often. For now, though, they were happy to try out different accommodations on their vacation trips.

This would be Kendi's first time in Chelan without her parents, and she was beyond excited. Her parents had worked it out with Kendi's school for her to miss the last two weeks of classes in Redmond because the tourist season began with Memorial Day weekend, and the summer workers needed to be trained and ready to hit the ground running when the tourists came to town.

Once Kendi's parents finished the tour of Aunty Nola's garden area, they said goodbye to the group. Kendi walked them out and gave them lots of hugs and a few tears as she waved goodbye to them.

"I'm really going to miss you guys," Kendi said with a sniffle. "I am so excited for this summer but I've never been away this long without you guys!"

"We will miss you too, cutie. But we will see you when we come later this summer! Until then, you can expect lots of calls," her mother warned.

"We'll miss all your fancy coffee drinks; we'll have to get some from you next time we come!" her dad chuckled as he waved out the window, and they drove away.

When Kendi came back into the house, Aunty Nola said, "Hey, Kendi, we were going to head over to pick up Hope at the bus station and get some dinner. Do you think you could be ready to go in ten minutes?"

"Absolutely!" Kendi replied. "Any special dress code?"

"No, darling. Chelan is very casual, even at the nicest restaurants. It is part of the beach town charm," Aunty Nola assured the girls, who had gathered around her to listen. "Sundresses or shorts are appropriate attire everywhere."

Ten minutes later, the girls were freshened up, dressed in their casual attire, and buckled into Aunty Nola's comfortable white van driving down main street toward the bus station.

Upon arrival, the three girls eagerly observed several groups of people debarking from a long shiny grey bus. They scanned the crowd to try to determine who would be their new housemate. The last girl exited the bus, and they all knew that must be Hope. She wore athletic shorts and a t-shirt with a Nike emblem on it. She had her hair in a long, dark blonde ponytail, and her blue eyes looked around expectantly.

Aunty Nola got out and greeted her. They had met via Facetime when Hope interviewed for her place in The Guesthouse, so they each knew what the other looked like. They exchanged pleasantries about the bus ride, and the girls got out of the car soon after to meet Hope.

They headed to Stillwaters Restaurant at Amie's family's resort for a first night welcome dinner with a good-natured warning from Aunty Nola that future dinners wouldn't be as fancy because it would mostly be good old-fashioned home cooking back at The Guesthouse.

Hope was quiet during dinner—she was always shy around new people at first—but it was clear based on comments she made that she was a nice girl and would get along great with the others.

Hope told the other girls about her job with her Uncle Joe's personal watercraft rental business. Uncle Joe had come to Chelan when he was a teenager and worked the summer seasons for many summers throughout both high school and college. He eventually was able to buy the small watercraft rental business from his former boss by making regular payments for several years. Uncle Joe lived frugally by renting a room in someone's home, had never married, and was able to build the business into a thriving enterprise that included both Jet Skis and boat rentals. For years, Hope had been looking forward to working for Uncle Joe. She was glad that she was finally old enough to make her own money and relieve some of the financial pressure that her mom felt.

In her spare time, she planned to keep in shape for soccer in the fall by running each morning.

"Which sports do you do?" Kendi asked Hope.

"I love most sports, but since I can only do one school sport per season, I do soccer, basketball, and track at school, play tennis at my local recreation center, and do a lot of running on my own." Hope responded proudly. "What do all of you like to do?"

"I like music," Kendi said, her green eyes shining, "I play a couple instruments and sing. I also love hanging out at coffee shops, so I was *so* excited that I landed this job at Brandon's Coffee and Bakeshop. I also love art, so I might be a designer someday, but who knows?"

"Wow! That's cool, Kendi. I am terrible at art and music," Emma said ruefully. "But I do like learning about business. I am actually starting a business blog, but I don't have any followers yet," she admitted. "I'll be working at the general store this summer. Mr. Femley told me it will be super busy, but he will find time to teach me things about the business in between stocking, working at the register, and serving ice cream cones. I think it'd be so cool to own a store someday. Maybe this will help me see the good and bad points. Plus, I'm really excited to just spend time on the lake this summer!"

"Me, too!" Amie agreed. "Even though I've lived here my whole life, hanging at the lake will never get old."

"I don't get it. If you already live here, why are you staying at The Guesthouse?" Hope inquired.

"My parents are going to be gone this summer, so they're renting our house to tourists while they're in Montana helping out my grandpa. He's recovering from a back injury. They thought that living at The Guesthouse would be a good experience for me since they have known Aunty Nola forever."

During dinner, the girls' lively conversation was interrupted frequently with people walking by and greeting Aunty Nola. Several of them stopped to be introduced to the girls.

"I'm getting the sense that everyone in the town of Chelan knows you, Aunty Nola. They all seem to know about The Guesthouse and that you take in four students each summer," Emma remarked.

"Oh yes, EVERYONE knows Aunty Nola. And everyone loves her, too, because she's so kind!" Amie explained. "She's one of the founding members of our church."

"Well, I know that I am not acquainted with *everybody* in town," Nola laughed a little, "but I have lived here a very long time and I am nosy enough that I want to get to know as many people as I can. It is fun to meet folks. I like to bring welcome baskets to new families that move here so I can hear their story. Everyone has a story, and it is so fun to find each one," she enthused.

Just then, an attractive African-American lady in her late twenties dressed in tailored navy shorts and a white golf shirt came over to greet Aunty Nola. She leaned down to give her a hug, then Aunty Nola introduced her to the girls as her friend Shayna.

Shayna smiled broadly and spoke to the girls. "Did you girls know that Aunty gets dozens of requests to stay in The Guesthouse each summer? She always handpicks who gets the four spots. It will be the best summer of your life! I know because I stayed there one summer when I was in high school and I enjoyed it so much, I ended up making Chelan my home after college. I am the marketing director at the golf course now. Have a great summer, ladies!" she said with a smile to the whole table before she walked away.

"I think we are lucky to be the ones chosen to be in The Guesthouse this summer," Hope contemplated.

"I don't know about that, but I do know that I am very happy to host all of you," Aunty Nola assured her. "Also, Amie, you haven't gotten a chance to share yet."

"Well," Amie started, "my great-grandpa on my dad's side was the one who started the Lakeshore Resort back about 80 years ago. My aunt and uncle manage it now, and my mom is the accountant. My dad is also involved. I've helped around the resort before, but this year is the first year that I'm old enough to officially be an employee. I'm super excited!"

"What do you like to do for fun?" Kendi asked her.

"I like to go wakeboarding and swimming. I love to lie out in the sun, and go shopping and buy clothes and shoes when I have extra money. I have different nail polish colors for every outfit. I love to color coordinate everything. I guess I'm pretty girly. I think for a career, I'd love to do something fashion related." Amie replied with a shrug.

"Hope, what do you think you'll do after high school?" Emma jumped in.

"Well," Hope began slowly, "I'm hoping to get an athletic scholarship in either soccer or basketball, because that's the only way I'm going to get to go to college. After that, maybe I can be a physical therapist or an athletic trainer or something like that. I think it'd be fun to work with athletes and help them optimize their performance. Ultimately, it'd be pretty cool to work for a US Olympic team helping the athletes." Hope's blue eyes lit up at the prospect.

"Maybe you could *be* one of the athletes instead?" Amie commented.

"That's probably a little out of my reach," Hope remarked, "but just to be able to make a living being around sports would be exciting for me."

The girls and Aunty Nola talked a long time and consumed several refills of their sparkling lemon cucumber water as the restaurant emptied out.

One thing that the girls–and all students past and future–agreed to when staying at The Guesthouse was that they would attend church every Sunday morning. Aunty Nola reminded them that tomorrow they would leave for church at 8:45 a.m. Later on Sunday evening, the high school group would have their annual pre-summer party where the kids could all get together before the crazy summer season kept a lot of them too busy to attend the regular weekly get-togethers. Amie assured the girls that they would not want to miss this party because the food would be amazing, the live music was crazy-good, and there would be a couple hundred teenagers there. Kendi and Emma eagerly anticipated meeting lots of other teens who would be hanging around Chelan this summer but Hope didn't like crowds or meeting new people, so this would be a challenge for her. She thought about making up an excuse not to attend but she decided to bite the bullet and go to this one.

Aunty Nola pulled the van into the driveway in front of The Guesthouse. The excited girls got out of the van and went upstairs to organize their rooms, catch up on social media, and figure out what they were going to wear for church and the beach party tomorrow night.

Judy Ann Koglin

CHAPTER TWO
First Sunday Morning

The next morning, the girls were ready to go promptly at 8:45 a.m..

Amie had spent her morning ironing a cute lavender outfit for church and selecting a matching purse and nail polish, which she carefully allowed to dry as best she could while she finished getting ready.

Hope had gone for an early morning run and had taken a shower, so her long hair was still a little damp. She had grabbed a granola bar from the glass jar that Aunty Nola kept on the counter next to the bowl of fresh fruit.

Kendi was up early chatting with Aunty Nola as they enjoyed a bowl of oatmeal with strawberries and coffee from the single-serve coffee maker.

Emma was the last to make it downstairs. She selected a banana for the road, and soon after everyone was assembled and ready. Hope worried that her gray yoga pants with a long light blue tunic might be a little too casual for church but she hoped it would be ok.

Kendi wore white linen capris and a green short-sleeved sweater, and Emma wore her favorite denim skirt with a dressy red scoop-neck t-shirt. Aunty Nola looked younger than her seventy years in comfortable grey slacks and a light pink button-down blouse. The five of them walked the four blocks to church together.

Hope wasn't sure what to expect. She had only been to an ornate Catholic church once for a wedding and had attended a really small church in Lynnwood with one of the girls from her soccer team a few times. She was pretty sure this wouldn't be like either of those churches, and she was right, because when they arrived, there were about 100 cars in the parking lot. It looked like several families were walking to church like they were.

The girls seated themselves in a row half way up on the right side of the church. Aunty Nola walked around and greeted lots of people before she joined the girls.

The service started out with an energetic young pastor coming up to the microphone. He said he was the youth pastor. He welcomed everyone, and then he reminded them that the annual beginning of summer beach party for high school students was tonight. The girls exchanged glances and then looked around to see how many other high school students might be there. Kendi could count about twenty kids who were probably in high school sitting in the rows in front of them and figured there were probably just as many behind them but she didn't want to turn around to look. The worship band came on the stage and they played and sang some upbeat songs. Fortunately, the words showed up on the two large screens on the sides of the stage so the girls could at least try to sing along. Hope felt pretty awkward during singing but she just mouthed the words and didn't think anyone would know the difference. After that, the head pastor came on stage and gave a good message about forgiveness. Aunty Nola took lots of notes in a notebook that she had brought with her. Amie was typing a lot on her phone and the other girls initially thought she was texting during the service and thought that might be in poor taste. However, they soon figured out by watching her reactions during key points of the sermon that she was just taking notes on an app. Emma thought that this preacher was a lot easier to listen to than other ones at churches she had occasionally attended in the past. Kendi and Hope listened quietly to the sermon and they seemed to be really interested with what the speaker was saying, even though they didn't understand a few of the things he talked about. After he finished, the younger pastor came up again and gave a few more announcements and then it was time to leave.

After church, the girls hung out in the lobby area, and Amie introduced them to a lot of her friends from school. She walked up to a small group of girls who looked about her age. "Hi ladies! You know that I am staying at The Guesthouse this summer. I wanted to introduce you to my roommates. Amie made a gesture to incorporate her roommates as she introduced them. "This is Emma, Kendi, and Hope and these girls," she continued, pointing to her local friends, "are Lexi, Amanda, and Hailey." Lexi was a beautiful Korean girl of medium height and slender build. Amanda had a round figure and a welcoming smile. She had shoulder-length brown hair with bangs. Hailey had dark blonde hair and green eyes and was pretty quiet. Emma seemed really excited to meet the local girls, Kendi was less exuberant but glad to meet them as well, and Hope felt really awkward because she was not good at small talk.

"Welcome to Chelan, y'all!" Amanda drawled with an accent that revealed her Southern roots. "Where are all of you from and where are you working this summer?"

Emma explained, "I am working at Mr. Femley's General Store, Kendi is working at the coffee shop, and Hope is working at her uncle's boat rental place."

"How about you girls?" Kendi asked.

The other girls discussed where they worked and the merits of each of their jobs. After about a half hour of chatting, Aunty Nola was finally able to extract herself from all her friends and was ready to go, and they walked back to The Guesthouse.

Hope had already arranged to meet her Uncle Joe for lunch at the hamburger place, so she took off on foot toward the lake. The rest of the group went back towards The Guesthouse to eat sandwiches and coleslaw.

After lunch, the girls went their separate ways; Emma and Kendi went on a walk together to explore town and stop by the places where they would start work tomorrow. Amie stopped by the resort because she had promised her aunt that she would help put together packets for the summer staff orientation that started tomorrow.

◊ ◊◊◊ ◊

Amie had helped her aunt do the orientation for last year's summer staff and she enjoyed it. Aunt Debbie was extremely organized and efficient and had all the copies made and laid out in the right order. Amie knew from what she had overheard from her parents that the resort was flourishing under Debbie and Bob's management. "They are both equally good managing people and projects so we are fortunate to have them at the helm," Amie's dad Randy had often commented. Amie was proud of her aunt and uncle but also of her parents who both did a great job in their positions. Overall, they were a good team to run the resort and it showed in the number of repeat guests they attracted.

When Amie arrived at the resort, her Aunt Debbie was dressed in jeans and a Lakeshore Resort sweatshirt with her medium-length brown hair pulled through the opening in the back of a baseball cap, looking much different than her usual businesslike appearance. She had explained previously that, in addition to assembling packets, they were also going to be hauling out the white plastic tables and chairs from storage and setting them up for Monday's new employee orientation session.

When Aunt Debbie saw Amie walk in, she stood up and greeted her with a hug and asked her lots of questions about The Guesthouse and her housemates. "Well, tell me all about it! How are things going?"

Amie reported, "So far, so good! They are all really nice and we all get along great. We all are really different, though."

"That is what's fun about summers here," Aunt Debbie mused. "You get to meet a lot of different people beyond the same folks who live here year-round. It never gets old for me, even though summers are so exhausting!" she laughed.

"Yeah. I'm so happy that I get to help out–I mean, really *work* at the resort this year...officially. By the way, have you decided what you're going to do with me?"

"Yes. I think we are going to have a need on the front desk crew for the first month. One of the ladies who always helps out during summer season just found out that she is not going to be able to come this year because she needs to help her mother with a move. All that being said, I was glad we hadn't locked you into a spot yet, so we can get you trained on the front desk this week. When people start rolling in on Thursday and Friday, we will be fully staffed up there." Debbie said enthusiastically.

"Oh, good! I think I'll love that spot! So, will I get to participate in orientation tomorrow morning? I heard that the cooks are serving an amazing breakfast for new staff tomorrow," Amie added.

"Yes, you'll do the first part of orientation. Then, you will head to the front desk at 11 o' clock, and Helen will begin your training. You will be a great asset because you know so much about this property already, and you have such a great personality for a first impression for guests. We're lucky to have you." Debbie gushed.

"Well, I guess I know the right people," Amie laughed. "If we're finished with these packets, I guess I'll take off, because I have the party to get ready for."

"Oh, definitely! Have fun tonight!"

"See ya tomorrow morning!" Amie called over her shoulder to her aunt.

◊ ◊◊◊ ◊

Just down the road a half mile, Hope was spending time with her Uncle Joe. He had taken her to Mike's Big Burgers, a local hamburger drive-in. After they finished their lunch, they went back to his office shack so she could learn a little bit about the business before she officially started the next day.

"I can't get over how much you look like your mother did at your age, except for your height. I'm glad she let you come this year," Joe smiled as he picked up a soapy rag in his sun-weathered hand and washed the side of one of his speedboats.

"I am, too. It'll be nice to hang out with you and make some money to take some of the burden off Mom. Thank you so much for paying my rent at The Guesthouse so I can be here this summer," Hope said gratefully.

"It was the least that I could do since I don't have anywhere you can stay. By the way, how are things going over there? What do you think of your roommates? I heard that the lady who runs the place is a great person."

"She really is. My roommates all seem nice, too. We're all going to be working at different places, and it sounds like we'll all be really busy this summer." Hope absentmindedly picked up another rag and started cleaning the front of the boat.

"I don't know about them and their jobs, but I know that I will be keeping you extremely busy. From what you told me, though, you wouldn't mind a little bit of overtime, right?" Uncle Joe teased.

"Nope! The more, the better! I'll be your hardest-working crew member this summer," Hope replied enthusiastically.

"That wouldn't surprise me a bit. You are just like your mom," Joe remarked.

That last comment took Hope by surprise because she never thought of herself to be anything like her mom.

Her mom Megan was much shorter than she was, and not very athletic. She had similar coloring with her eyes and hair, but Hope didn't see a resemblance at all, although others sometimes did. Megan worked at a manufacturing plant and another part-time retail job on weekends. Hope had always looked forward to the time where she would be old enough to finally get a part-time job and help out. Even though her mom had never, ever complained, Hope knew that all her sports fees

34

and equipment were the reason that her mom had to work the extra job. So, when Uncle Joe told them that she could work all summer and get lots of hours, she jumped at the chance.

"Hope, are you going to that high school beach party tonight? They are renting some of our equipment."

"I don't know. The girls in our house are going, and they're really excited about it, but...parties aren't really my thing." Hope explained.

"I'm not telling you what you should do, but why don't you go and check it out? We have a lot of great kids in this town, and it would be nice for you to meet a few before you are stuck here every day."

"Maybe I will. I'd better head back now if I'm gonna go to this thing tonight. I'll see you first thing in the morning," Hope said brightly.

"Actually, there is no rush to do training and I'll probably go for a run in the morning. Why don't we meet here around 9 o' clock, and we can get you up to speed. Things won't really start brewing here with customers until at least Thursday, since that is the day before Memorial Day weekend. At that point, you'd better buckle your seatbelt!"

"Sounds good, Uncle Joe! See you tomorrow at 9."

And with that, Hope jogged home. It was nice to spend time with Uncle Joe. He was so level-headed and thoughtful. Hope had heard he was an athlete back in the day, but she didn't know any of those details yet.

◊ ◊◊◊ ◊

35

After lunch at The Guesthouse, while Amie was getting acquainted with her resort work and Hope was catching up with her uncle, Emma and Kendi took a walk to see each other's places of employment.

The first stop was Brandon's Coffee and Bakeshop, where Kendi would be working.

Emma's heart skipped a beat when she saw a tall, blond boy behind the counter. She whispered to Kendi mischievously, "Is it too late to switch jobs with you?"

Kendi laughed and said, "Let's order some coffee."

They stepped up to the counter. Kendi ordered and paid for a double-shot caramel latte with skim milk, then stepped aside for Emma to place her order. Emma stumbled over her order for an iced mocha because she was nervous talking to the good-looking cashier. She was trying to make some witty small talk with him but couldn't think of anything to say.

Luckily, he started a conversation with the two girls. He told them his name was Ben, and he asked them if they were just passing through, or if they were staying in Chelan.

Kendi shared that they were there for the summer, introducing herself and Emma and sharing a little bit about how they were staying at The Guesthouse. She then revealed that she was actually going to be his coworker starting tomorrow and he smiled.

"My dad told me that we were going to have a couple new staff training with us tomorrow, but he didn't mention who they were," said Ben. He turned to Emma. "Are you another new summer staff member?"

"Yes...well, no...well, yes. I *am* here to work, but not here at the coffee shop," Emma stammered. "I'm working as a clerk at Femley's General Store starting tomorrow."

"Oh, you'll like it there," Ben said knowingly. "Mr. Femley is really nice and treats his staff very well–"

"Wait." Kendi broke in, "You said your dad told you about the new trainees. Is your dad Mr. Brandon?"

"Well, his name is Mark Brandon. Did he tell you the story about this place when you interviewed?"

"No! Do you have time to tell us now?" Kendi asked.

"Sure! It's pretty quiet now, and I'm going to be closing up for the day anyway. We're just open on Sundays until the after-church crowd comes through, then I shut it down unless we're doing an event on a Sunday night. Pull up a chair, and I'll tell you the story."

As the girls were situating themselves, Ben went and flipped the sign in the door so the "Closed" side would be visible to passersby. He then joined the girls at the table.

"So," Ben began, "my dad and mom were high school sweethearts here in Chelan. They went off to college, and my mom majored in Corporate Communications while my dad studied to become an electrical engineer. They went their separate ways but stayed friends.

"After college, both of them got great jobs, mom in Seattle and dad in the Tri-Cities, so they were in different parts of the state and never saw each other. They didn't have social media or even texting then. A couple years later, they saw each other again at the midnight Christmas Eve church service here in Chelan. They went down to the boat docks afterwards to talk and decided that they wanted to be together. They got married just one week later on New Year's Eve.

"They kept their jobs on opposite sides of the state, and saw each other on weekends. They saved all their money for a year and a half, then moved back here and rented a small house, using the money they'd saved to start this coffee shop-slash-bakery. Soon, they had my brother Joseph, and then they had me, and we pretty much grew up here. My mom Rachel likes to bake, so she runs the bakery part, and my dad is in charge of the coffee shop. My brother is an insane musician, so he runs the special events, and I just help where needed. We have a couple other ladies, Lynn and Bonnie, who also work here. Every year, we hire a couple more people for the season."

"Wow, this place has a cool backstory," Emma commented. "It would be a fun story to write about someday. I'm actually from the Tri-Cities, too…Pasco, actually. My dad works out in the Hanford area and my family owns a winery."

"That's cool," Ben remarked. "I've been through there a couple times. It's beautiful with the Columbia River and the hills." Then, turning to Kendi, he asked, "Are you ready to work tomorrow?"

"I'm ready! When's the next music night?" she asked.

"We'll have entertainment on both Friday and Saturday night this weekend. Are you musical, Kendi?"

"A little bit. I like to sing and can play the guitar and piano a little," Kendi said humbly.

"How about you, Emma?" Ben turned his attention to her.

"I'm more of a cheerleader for those of you who can perform. I'm a great audience." Emma laughed.

"Well, good. I hope you join us for our special events. Oh, by the way, did anyone invite you to the beach party tonight?"

"Yeah, we'll definitely be there!" Kendi confirmed. "In fact, we'd better get going because we wanted to stop by the general store, too. See you tonight!"

The girls went out the front door and waved at Ben as he locked up after them and finished cleaning up the store.

Femley's General Store was only about a block away from Brandon's Coffee and Bakeshop, and the girls chatted away excitedly as they made the short walk.

"Oh my goodness, Ben is so ah-mazing. I wonder if he is about our age. He's *so* good-looking and really friendly, too. I wonder if he has a girlfriend?" Emma questioned.

"I don't know, but it looks like it'll be a fun place to work with all the music events!" Kendi enthused as they walked.

A few moments later, they arrived at the store, and the girls spent some time walking around checking out the assortment of beachwear, brightly colored beach towels, and fun floatation devices. The girls agreed that they had all the things needed for a day at the lake.

Mr. Femley was not in the store that day, so they didn't get to chat with him. Still, Emma made a point to introduce herself to a smiling middle-aged lady named Tricia who was stocking the flip flops which were hung on a rack close to the front of the store. Tricia walked Emma back to the ice cream counter in the back of the store and introduced her to another lady named Kim. Emma took an immediate liking to both of these ladies.

In the meantime, Kendi had found a swimsuit cover up that would match one of her bikinis really well, so the girls went up to the register to buy it. The lady at the counter, Ellen, was in a bit of a hurry since there were several customers, but Emma quickly introduced herself and told Ellen that she would see her tomorrow.

◊ ◊◊◊ ◊

Emma and Kendi made their return back to The Guesthouse to get ready for the party. When they arrived, Hope and Amie were already there, the latter of the two, second guessing what to wear for the third time.

"What are you going to wear, Hope?" Amie asked.

Hope shrugged, "I guess I was going to wear what I have on," she admitted, pointing to the yoga pants and light blue shirt she had worn to church that morning.

"How would you feel about wearing one of my dresses?" Amie asked carefully so as not to offend.

"Um, I'm really not a dress person but if that is what we are supposed to wear, I guess it would be okay. But I am *a lot* taller than you."

Amie looked in her closet, now tightly packed with outfits, and selected a green and white sundress that looked longer than the rest. "How about this one?" Amie asked.

Hope breathed a sigh of relief. "Yeah, that will be okay, I guess. I was hoping you wouldn't pull out anything pink."

"No, I promise that I wouldn't do that to you," Amie laughed.

Hope was used to changing in front of other girls in the locker room so she quickly changed into the pretty green sundress. She had to admit it looked good on her and wasn't too short."

"Wow, that looks perfect," Amie remarked. "Now, what about your hair?"

"Um, what about it?" Hope asked, pulling her ponytail to the front of her shoulder somewhat defensively.

Again, Amie treaded lightly. "Your hair is so long and pretty. How would you feel about me blowing it out and curling it a little bit? I know it would be gorgeous."

"Ok, I guess," Hope replied. She was never interested in this girly stuff but for some reason, she trusted Amie and knew that she probably needed to up her style game anyway."

Hope sat down in front of the vanity and Amie sprayed water in her hair as well as a heat protectant and blew her hair out using a round brush to add some curl. By now Kendi and Emma had wandered in.

"Oh my gosh – you look beautiful!" Emma blurted.

Kendi gave Hope an unopened pink lip gloss from her stash and some sandals that were a little too big for her but fit Hope perfectly. Emma gave Hope a bracelet to wear that looked perfect with the green dress she had borrowed from Amie.

Hope looked in the mirror and admitted to herself that she actually looked pretty good, even if she was feeling really uncomfortable with all the attention. She knew they meant well and they were really nice.

The other girls finished getting themselves ready, Amie wore a red and white striped sundress with a white headband, Kendi wore a dusty pink romper and put her thick wavy red hair in a high ponytail, and Amie wore a royal blue sundress that drew attention to her bright blue eyes.

"You girls all look gorgeous," Aunty Nola gushed when they came downstairs. They loaded up the van and drove the short distance to the entrance of the park. "I will pick you ladies up here at 10:30 p.m. If you want to come home earlier, just give me a call."

CHAPTER THREE
Beach Party

When the girls got to the registration table that the church had set up, they signed in with their local address. Amie had explained to them earlier that the event was sponsored by the church, but it was open to all the high schoolers of the town, regardless of whether they went to church. In past years, there were incidents of people from neighboring towns crashing the party and harassing the kids, so they put in security measures to make sure that attendance was limited to incoming freshmen through outgoing seniors only, along with pre-approved chaperones.

The other girls saw Amie as a good resource because she was well-known by most of the people there. Amie, meanwhile, was delighted to spend time introducing her new housemates to others.

They ran into two guys who were on the track team at Chelan High named Brett and Conner, and Amie introduced Hope and the other girls to them. Brett, a tall, thin, and handsome African American guy had just

43

graduated, and Conner, also tall and thin but with light brown hair and brown eyes, would be a senior this coming year. "Brett and I are neighbors and we grew up playing together. Conner would come over to play with Brett and they would be annoyed by the little neighbor girl following them around but they still played with me," she explained. Hope asked them where they trained, and they struck up a good conversation about their preferred running trails.

After making some more brief small talk, Amie and the other girls excused themselves and left Hope to chat with Brett and Conner for a while.

Then, Amie ran into a group of her friends from school and she introduced Emma and Kendi to them. They chatted for a bit about where they were all planning to work this summer. One of the girls, Ashley, actually worked in the General Store year-round but only worked on the weekends during the school year.

"Any tips you can give me?" Emma asked her.

"I have lots of them," Ashley said, taking a sip of fruit punch. "I'll help you out, no problem." She took another swallow of punch before she gave the same tips she always gave the newcomers: "First rule: don't get on Ellen's bad side. She can get a little cranky, but stay on her good side, and she will have your back."

"Okay, so be nice to Ellen–check," Emma repeated. "Tell me more! What other things should I know?"

"Mr. Femley is the best," Ashley told her earnestly. "He is so patient with all of us. Tell you what, let's grab some food, and I'll tell you more about what we do at the store," Ashley replied and the two of them headed to the buffet tables to get hot dogs, leaving Kendi and Amie behind.

Kendi and Amie walked by the band that was playing a variety of music. Kendi thought it was kind of like listening to the contestants on some of the TV singing contests once they had arrived at the top ten, because the songs were all different but they were all crowd-pleasers. They had just played a mash-up of beach-themed songs, some country and some surfer music from the sixties. Kendi was impressed with their arrangement and she asked Amie who they were. Amie told her the band was made up of four guys who used to go to Chelan High.

"You know Ben Brandon at the coffee shop?" Amie asked.

"...Yeah? Emma and I just met him today, actually. Why?"

"One of the guys is the Ben's older brother, Joseph," Amie revealed.

Kendi's eyes widened in surprise. "Oh! Okay! Ben mentioned that he had a brother who was a good musician." Now that Amie had pointed him out, she could definitely see the resemblance between the two guys.

Kendi really liked the band's sound. Amie explained that they had been playing together for years and got gigs all over the region. Sometimes they played at the coffee shop where Kendi was going to work, which made sense since the lead singer was the owners' son.

Kendi and Amie went through the buffet line and grabbed hot dogs, a watermelon slice, potato salad, and a cookie. After they got their dinner, Kendi said she thought she would like to sit in the chairs by the band and eat. She assured Amie that she would be fine by herself and released Amie from her hostess duties so she could go hang out with her local friends.

Kendi was really enjoying the music and almost didn't notice when a male voice said, "Hi Kendi!"

Kendi looked up and saw Ben, the only male in town who knew her name so far. He was wearing white shorts with a navy blue polo and some deck shoes. He looked exactly how Kendi would picture a classy guy at a beach party.

"Hi, Ben!" she said enthusiastically. "I was just enjoying your brother's band. I was wondering if I would run into you."

"Yeah! A lot of people show up at this party every year, and it gets pretty crowded, so I didn't know if I would see you. By the way, where's your sidekick?"

"All of my housemates are here. I last saw Emma in the food line."

Just then, a group of Ben's friends showed up, and they greeted each other with some kind of mix between a high-five and a hand clasp. The boys were a variety of heights and builds but they all looked like they were happy to meet Kendi. He introduced them to Kendi. "Kendi, this is Tyson, Cody, Tanner, Ryan, and Dylan. Guys, this is Kendi. She is from Redmond."

Dylan, a short muscular guy with dark features said,

"Trust Ben to meet all the pretty new girls in town the first day they're here." The other guys nodded in agreement.

Kendi replied spunkily, "Well, it's actually my second day here."

"Well, Ben must be slipping then! By the way where are you working this summer, Kendi?" Tyson, a medium height boy with reddish-blond hair asked curiously.

"Actually, I'm working at Brandon's with Ben," Kendi replied with a smile.

"Hmmm, looks like I'm going to have to become a coffee drinker this summer," the tallest guy in the group teased. Kendi blushed from the compliment. "Hey Kendi, it was very nice to meet you! Hopefully we'll see each other around?"

Dylan, Cody, Tyson, and Tanner heard one of the adults summoning them to move some tables that the ladies in charge of the food were struggling with, so they waved goodbye to Kendi and they jogged across the grass to help carry the tables.

Kendi turned her attention to the tall boy with chestnut brown hair and sparkling brown eyes who lingered. "Sounds really great. Ummm…I'm sorry, I guess I didn't catch your name," Kendi stammered.

"It's Ryan," he replied. He gave Kendi a dazzling smile and jogged up the grassy hill to catch up with his group. Kendi had to catch her breath after that because Ryan was probably one of the best looking guys she had ever talked with one-on-one.

She turned her attention back to Ben, who was no slouch, either. The two of them had a good time talking but, after about ten minutes, Ben heard some of his guy friends yelling for him to join their team for a beach volleyball game. He seemed torn between hanging out with Kendi and the irresistible urge to join the game and the insistent calls from the volleyball players won the battle. "I guess I'll see ya at work, Kendi. Have fun tonight!"

"Sounds good, see ya later!" Kendi wasn't sure what she thought of Ryan and Ben. Ryan certainly was the definition of tall, dark, and handsome and Ben was also tall and handsome but with tousled beachy blond hair with blue eyes. She wondered if she would have a chance to talk with Ryan more this summer. She knew that she would definitely have more time to get to know Ben. *What's gotten into you, Kendi? You are sounding as boy-crazy as Bella!*

Her musings were cut short when someone plopped down next to her. She looked over and was pleased to see that it was Hope. She explained that the guys she had met, Conner and Brett, liked to run in the morning before it got too hot out, and she got their numbers and might meet up with them to run sometime.

"They also told me about some good running trails!" Hope told her. "What about you? "Have you met anyone here, Kendi?"

"A few people. I just heard the announcer say that they are doing competitive games in the grassy area. Do you want to go over there?"

"Sure!" Hope said.

Hope and Kendi headed over to the grassy area and met up with Emma and Amie. The announcer said they were going to do the competitive games and proceeded to split them up into four teams.

Hope, Amie, Emma, and Kendi were all assigned to the red team, and each person on the team had to participate in one of the games.

Hope and Kendi were assigned a relay-type event where each participant took their turn kicking a soccer ball through a series of cones, then turning around and kicking the ball through the cones going in the opposite direction and passing the ball to the next person.

Hope went first and navigated the cones like a pro, even though she wished she wasn't wearing a dress and sandals for this event. Kendi went after her and found that she was going up against Ben, who was on the yellow team, and Conner, who was on the blue team. Kendi had a slight head start due to Hope's stellar performance, but she and the subsequent participants from the red team were not able to keep the lead, and the red team finished third in that event.

Emma was matched up with her new coworker Ashley for her game. She was blindfolded, and her partner had to guide her through an obstacle course using only voice commands. The two girls played well and narrowly missed a first place finish in their event.

Amie's event was to attempt to throw a football through a hanging tire at varying distances. The announcer explained that you would have three attempts to make your shot from 12 feet away and, if you made your shot in one of your three attempts, you were moved five yards back and got to try three times from that mark.

It was a bit of a losing battle for Amie because she was so small, but she gamely stepped up and gave it her best shot, and her third throw went through the tire to the loud cheers and applause of her teammates. She moved back to the next mark and tried but unfortunately, she missed all three attempts, and her team tied for third place in the football toss event.

In the end, the red team did not win the competition, but they did win the Spirit Award for cheering the loudest and being the most supportive of each other. The girls were happy that they at least were able to take home that title.

After the competition, everyone gathered at the beach and watched the sunset. The band resumed playing, and the four girls found seats together in the back row of folding chairs. It was a warm evening, and the breeze off the lake was perfect. The music was great, and the girls were having a great time getting to know each other.

Pretty soon, some of Amie's friends from school came over and told her that the bonfire was ready if she and all her roommates were interested in making s'mores. The girls agreed that they were definitely ready for that and headed over to the table to grab marshmallows and sticks.

When they were roasting their marshmallows, some

of their new friends showed up. Ben and Ryan came over to where the girls were toasting marshmallows, and they were introduced to Hope and Emma. They already knew Amie from school, but they didn't know that she was living at The Guesthouse this summer. She explained her housing situation with a laugh. Conner and Brett also came by and hung out with the girls.

One of the guys on the stage spoke into the mic, and everyone grew quiet. He explained that the church sponsors this gathering every year before the Memorial Weekend crowd comes and ushers in the busy season. He invited everyone to come check out their Sunday services sometime this summer.

"Thank you all for coming out tonight! Please go out in the world and shine your light this summer to all the vacationers!"

Once the mic was turned off, everyone said goodbye to each other and went their separate ways. Aunty Nola was waiting in her van to pick them up, and the girls chatted nonstop about the fun they had.

◊ ◊◊◊ ◊

When they got home, Aunty Nola wanted each girl to tell them their favorite part.

"My favorite part was all the cute boys," Emma said with a giggle. "I'm not sure who I like the best yet."

Hope remarked that she was glad that she met some runners to help her find trails for early morning runs.

Amie said it was fun to see her friends outside of school.

"What was your favorite part, Kendi?" Aunty Nola asked.

Kendi answered slowly, "I guess I was surprised how many nice kids were there. I don't have too many friends back home except my best friend Bella. The kids here seem different. They're really welcoming and kind."

"I think you are right, my dear," Aunty Nola said nodding, "We do have a large percentage of really nice people in Chelan. It might be because of the spirit of gratitude people feel getting to live so close to this amazing lake. It also might be the small-town friendliness. Whatever, it is, I feel very blessed to live here, and I am so happy you girls get to experience a summer here. It may actually change your life."

The girls thought that might be a bit dramatic, but all of them were open to the possibility of good things happening this summer.

That night, all four girls slept really well with special memories floating through their minds.

CHAPTER FOUR
Starting Work

As usual, Hope was up before the sun. She threw on some shorts and a t-shirt, pulled her long hair back in a ponytail, and laced up her running shoes. She was excited to try out a running trail that Conner had told her about yesterday. She quietly closed the front door of The Guesthouse behind her so as not to wake up the others and did some stretches in the front lawn.

She jogged about a half mile to the trailhead. While she jogged, she reflected about the beach party last night. In retrospect, she was glad she went, but if it had been left up to her, she would not have gone and would certainly not have dressed up and curled her hair. She much preferred to stay out of the spotlight and do her own thing.

Going into the summer, she had discussed the subject with her mom before she'd even set foot on that bus to Chelan.

"Hope," her mom had said, "there are probably going to be times this summer where you have to make a choice to do things you aren't especially comfortable because you are part of a group. Please challenge yourself to get out of your comfort zone a little bit, because you might find that you like more things than you thought. However, this does NOT apply to drinking, drugs, and boys!" she quickly added with a laugh.

Hope laughed at the memory as she ran against the wind. Her mom was a selfless person, determined to give Hope the best life she could possibly provide. Hope appreciated all the sacrifices her mom had made. Her mom wanted nothing more than for Hope to go to college, get a great job, get married, and have a family. Hope respected her mom so much and did everything she could to lighten the load for her.

Thinking back to the beach party and how awkward she felt when Amie and Kendi were fixing her up, she was surprised to find that she did not mind the end result. She wouldn't want to do that every day, but every now and then might not be so bad.

She was startled out of her reminiscing when a male voice commented out of nowhere, "Hey Hope! I was hoping I would run into you." She looked up to see Conner, one of the boys she talked with at the beach party. He had arrived at the trailhead at the same time as she did, and was dressed for a run with his green and grey Chelan High cross country warm ups on. He had messy hair and Hope could barely hear some bass music thumping out of his white earbuds.

"Oh! Hi, Conner! I thought I'd get a couple miles in before I needed to start work."

"Want to run together?" Conner asked expectantly.

"Sure!" Hope replied. She normally liked to run alone so she could go at her own pace, but she was not disappointed when Conner suggested they run together.

They started out slowly and talked a little as they ran, mostly about the trail and where their schools had gone for track meets. Hope had just finished her sophomore year, and Conner had finished his junior year. Their high schools were not close geographically, and they were in different divisions, so they determined that they had never run into each other at a track meet or an invitational.

The time passed quickly as they ran, and by the time they had reached the three-mile mark and got back to the start, they had found that they had a lot in common besides running.

"Hopefully we can run together again sometime," Conner said as he was getting into his car. "Hey, did you want me to drop you off at The Guesthouse?" he asked.

"No, that's okay. I'm fine. But I had fun today!" Hope assured him.

Once Conner drove off into the Chelan morning, Hope started jogging back to The Guesthouse with a new spring in her step that she couldn't really figure out.

◊ ◊◊◊ ◊

Hope arrived back at her room and wasted no time showering and changing. By then, Aunty Nola was in the kitchen. Aunty Nola had spent time with each girl on the phone before they came for the summer, talking about what the girls liked for breakfast, whether they were an early bird or a night owl, and any special dietary restrictions. She knew they would all be on different schedules. Her plan was that each girl could grab what they wanted from the kitchen for breakfast, she would be happy to pack them a lunch, or they could fend for themselves, and she would cook a meal for whichever girls were home for dinner. She would keep copies of each of the girls' work schedules on the refrigerator so she could somewhat keep track of who would be home for dinner. The girls promised to send a text if they had a change of plans.

Aunty Nola had a reasonable-but-comprehensive list of house rules, which she had sent to each girl in advance and had posted on the stainless steel fridge in the kitchen so everyone could be on the same page regarding expectations. She had thought of everything from the 10 o'clock curfew (with exceptions), meal planning to access codes for the door. Instead of issuing individual house keys, Aunty Nola had a 4-digit keypad on her door and issued each girl their own code, not to be shared. Thus, they could always be assured that the house was locked when they left and that they would have access upon their return. Also, no one had to carry keys with them when they went to the beach. It was apparent that this was not her first rodeo.

Not only did she have the rules to a science, but she also had rooming arrangements figured out based on the girls' schedules. She had placed Hope and Kendi's bedrooms with the shared bath on the left side of the hall because Hope got up early all the time by choice and Kendi would likely have a lot of early shifts at the bakery/coffee shop. Emma and Amie were paired up on the right side of the hall because they preferred to stay up later and sleep in when they didn't have to get up early for work.

Meanwhile, Kendi groaned briefly when her alarm went off at 5:30 a.m. She had planned it so she would maximize her sleep. She took a super-quick shower, then ran down the stairs, grabbed an apple, and almost ran out the door before she saw Aunty Nola with a paper cup and lid. "Girl can't go without coffee, can she?" Aunty Nola teased.

"Oh, thank you Aunty! You are the best ever!" Kendi called behind her as she hustled out the door.

◊ ◊◊◊ ◊

Kendi made it to Brandon's Coffee and Bakeshop promptly at 6:00 a.m.

She was greeted by one of her new bosses, Rachel Brandon, a pretty redhead in her early-mid-forties. Mark was behind the counter helping a couple of customers with their espresso orders. Kendi also noticed a petite Asian girl around her age with straight shiny black hair standing near Rachel.

"Kendi, it is nice to see you again," Rachel told her. "Reed, this is Kendi, who is from Redmond; Kendi, this is Reed, who is from Manson, not far from here. You will both be training today."

The girls shook hands and gave each other awkward smiles and hellos.

"So, girls," Rachel said, "the first thing we will have you do is your starting paperwork. Then, Reed, you will work with Mark on espresso for the next two days, and Kendi will work with me in the bakeshop side. Then, on Wednesday, you will switch. By Friday, you will both know enough to be dangerous," she laughed at their concerned faces. "Don't worry; there will always be one of us around to help out. My husband Mark is our espresso guru, and I do most of the baking. My son Ben helps out mostly with the coffee shop, and Joseph comes in later on days when we have special events. We also have a couple ladies who work here year-round. We gave them today off because we will need all hands on deck this weekend."

Kendi decided she was really going to like Rachel. She reminded her of her own mom – they were even both gingers.

They spent the day in the back room learning the different types of treats that they offered on a regular basis. Rachel showed her where the recipes were kept, and they made batches of mint brownies, almond croissants, and cowboy cookies. Rachel suggested that she try samples of everything they made so that she would be able to answer the customers' questions when they asked about the items. By lunchtime, Kendi knew two things. One–that she was going to like working here, and two–that she was glad she hadn't packed a lunch because she was full. She made a mental note to only taste smaller samples in the future.

Kendi was curious about whether Ben was going to come in today, but decided to just wait and see.

She had a half-hour for her lunch break, so she walked over to Mr. Femley's General Store to see what Emma was doing. Emma was shadowing Tricia and learning about the merchandise in the store.

Tricia saw Kendi and said, "Hey, Emma, since your friend is here, why you don't take a 10-minute break? I need to make a phone call."

Emma and Kendi scurried out to the sidewalk, and Emma immediately asked, "So…was he there?"

"Was who where?" Kendi asked innocently, pretending not to know what Emma was talking about.

"Ben, of course! Did you see him?" Emma said with exasperation in her voice.

"Um, I can't remember if he was there or not …" Kendi teased.

"How can you not remember? It isn't a very big place!"

"Oh, yeah … no, he wasn't there." Kendi revealed.

"Oh, bummer. You got up early for nothing!" Emma whined on her friend's behalf.

"It wasn't for nothing, it was for my job!" Kendi reminded her. "The fact that Ben will be there sometimes is just a little bonus. By the way, I've already had three items from the bakeshop. I'm going to have to get some larger clothes! How has your shift been?"

"It's been good. Just stocking shelves so far, but I'll learn the register later today. I'd better get back in there. I'll stop by on my lunch and get a coffee."

"Sounds good! See ya then." After saying goodbye to Emma, Kendi hurried back to work.

When she got back, she learned the best way to clean the cases, how to check on an order from the supply vendor, and where to store the supplies. She also learned how to check to make sure the proper temperatures were maintained in the walk-in freezer, the cooler and the refrigerated display case.

Kendi was surprised how much there was to learn, and the next few hours flew by. Before she knew it, Rachel said, "Well, it's 2:30. See you tomorrow."

Kendi looked at the clock because she couldn't believe time had passed that quickly. She thanked Rachel for the great day and said goodbye.

"Oh, wait," Rachel called as Kendi was going out the door. "I forgot that I was going to send some treats for Aunty Nola and the other girls." Rachel handed Kendi a bag with about a dozen different baked goods and sent her on her way.

Just then, Kendi saw Emma coming towards the shop. She had almost forgotten that Emma was coming to get a coffee. Kendi decided she wanted one too, so they walked in together and ordered drinks.

They sat outside at one of the tables and Kendi offered her one of the pastries from the bag. Emma had one of the cowboy cookies that Kendi had helped make, and Emma pronounced it delicious.

After a little more chitchat, Emma headed back to work, and Kendi started her walk back to The Guesthouse. When she was walking, she heard someone from a passing car say "Kendi!"

Kendi looked at the car which had pulled over to the curb. It was Ryan, the friend of Ben's that she had met at the beach party. He flashed her his amazing smile through the open car window and she came over to say hi. He was wearing a pair of red swim trunks and a white tank top with a red Slip and Slide logo on the left chest area.

"Hey, Ryan! How's it going?"

"Good! I was just heading to the bank. How was your first day of work?"

"It was good. I learned a lot about the bakeshop part of the business." Kendi replied, offering him one of the cookies. "Where are you working?"

"My parents own the Slip and Slide at the entrance to town," Ryan said, munching on the cookie.

"Really? I've been there lots of times with my parents through the years!"

"I have worked there since I was about ten years old. I did easy things when I was young, like collecting towels and folding them when they came out of the laundry. I graduated to stamping hands for re-entrance, then selling tickets, then, eventually, lifeguarding. Now, I'm the assistant manager, so I helped hire our staff, and I'm training them and taking care of issues that arise."

"Wow, that sounds like a lot of responsibility," Kendi offered her approval.

"It is, but my parents are still in charge, so they make the tough decisions. I just watch and learn." Ryan said humbly.

"Well, I bet you have a lot of stories to tell about the water park."

"I definitely do. Maybe we could go to dinner sometime, and I could entertain you with my stories?" Ryan winked at her.

Kendi blushed and stammered, "I-I'd better get going! Nice to see you, Ryan!"

"Bye, Kendi!" Ryan called after her, amused by her response.

◊ ◊◊◊ ◊

Meanwhile, at Joe's Jet Skis and Boat Rentals, Hope was learning about the various watercraft and how to fill out the rental forms and answer common questions.

Joe said that about half of Hope's responsibilities would likely be answering questions over the phone, scheduling reservations for the personal watercraft and boats, and having people sign waivers. When it was busy, she might also be receiving the Jet Skis from people as they returned them, making sure they didn't go over their allotted time and fill the gas tanks when needed. Hope was a fast learner, and Joe was impressed how quickly she grasped the new information.

"You'll be running this place by the end of the summer," Uncle Joe joked.

"We'll see…I haven't even worked with a customer yet," Hope protested.

"I can tell you're a natural," Joe assured her.

Just then, the phone rang, and Hope was able to take her first reservation of two Jet Skis with the help of Uncle Joe.

She spent the rest of her shift organizing the office space that had been dormant over the winter season and answering the occasional phone call.

"Hey Hope, I forgot to ask: how did the beach party go?" her uncle wanted to know.

"It was okay, I guess. Not really my thing, but I met some other runners, so that was kinda cool."

"Well, there are a lot of great kids in this town. You'll meet a couple of them later this week. I bring them in every summer for extra help. Anyway, it looks like it is quitting time, girl. Good job today! I'll see you tomorrow. Let's come in at 9 o' clock again tomorrow and Wednesday. Starting Thursday, we'll have to come in at 8 o' clock," Joe explained.

"Sounds good! See ya tomorrow, Uncle Joe!"

Judy Ann Koglin

CHAPTER FIVE
Sunset Gathering

When Hope arrived home, she was greeted with a wonderful smell of hot lasagna that had just come out of the oven. The other girls were hanging out in the kitchen, and Aunty Nola was pulling a fresh loaf of toasted garlic bread out of the oven.

Over dinner, everyone reported on their first day at work. All the girls agreed that they had enjoyed their day.

As Amie listened to the excited chatter, she was surprised how close she felt to the other girls already. It was like they were a little family. She was really glad that she had made the decision to stay at The Guesthouse this summer instead of going with her parents to Montana or pushing to stay by herself in their family home on the lake.

The girls helped put the food on the table, then Aunty Nola said grace. Following the blessing, Aunty Nola asked each of them to talk about their favorite part of the day as they ate.

Hope responded, "I was really excited to check out the running trail. It was so cool when we came around the bend and saw the amazing view of the lake!"

"Wait, what? Did you say 'we'?" Emma asked curiously as she passed the green beans. "Who were 'we' running with?"

"Well, um…when I got to the trail, Conner happened to be there, so I ran with him," Hope explained.

"Wow! Conner is a great guy. He is really popular at my school," Amie reported. "I'm not surprised you guys hit it off."

"Oh, it was just a run–no big deal!" Hope interjected. "By the way, this lasagna is delicious," she quickly deflected.

"You never know, Hope, he could be your summer boyfriend…" Emma said merrily. "And I agree, the lasagna is incredible!"

"Well, I had a fun day," Kendi said. "My favorite part was baking treats with Rachel Brandon. At first I was a little bit disappointed that they were training me in the bakeshop because I was more interested in the coffee shop, but I found out that baking is really fun! "And, by the way, I brought home a bag of fresh baked goods for all of you for dessert!"

"Awesome! I think you're going to be a great roommate to have!" Amie teased.

"I am always glad when I get to host someone who works at the bakeshop. They always have such tasty treats," Aunty Nola said with a laugh. "How about you, Amie? Did you have fun today?"

"Yes, I really did. It seemed weird going through orientation when I have been at the resort literally since I was a baby, but it was still fun. After I finished orientation stuff, I started training for my front desk duties. Even though I know a lot about the resort, I've never worked with the reservation and check-in software, so that's going to be a challenge. This is a good time to train because we had several check-ins, but it wasn't overwhelming like they said it will be on Thursday and Friday," Amie shared.

Emma took her turn: "I had fun at work today. I am learning every aspect of the store, so I don't think it'll get boring. They have super cute beach merchandise. I know the customers are going to love it. I know it'll be even more fun when the tourists start rolling in." Emma had such a bubbly personality that the others couldn't help to catch her joy.

"After we clean up the dishes, does anyone want to walk to the park and watch the sunset on the water?" Kendi asked.

The other girls chorused with "I do!"

Emma asked, "How about you, Aunty?"

"Oh, thank you for the invitation, but I have worship team practice tonight. By the way, if any of you girls like to sing, we can always use more singers. We all rehearse together, and then each mini group leads worship once a month," Aunty Nola encouraged.

"Hmm, I might be interested at some point. I do love to sing and my vocal chords probably need to be exercised a bit. I'll let you know," Kendi promised.

Aunty Nola had a chore chart on the fridge. Kendi and Emma were in charge of the dishes on Monday nights, and Hope and Amie would clean up after dinner on Tuesday. The girls finished up the dishes and headed to the lake for sunset.

◊ ◊◊◊ ◊

When the four girls arrived at the beach park, they were surprised to see many of the teens who were at last night's party. Amie introduced her housemates to some more of her friends. Then, they all watched a magnificent sunset that included beautiful shades of orange and pink.

"You haven't seen a sunset until you've seen one here," Amie boasted proudly.

"I agree. I always love the sunsets when we come to town," Kendi reminisced.

Just then, a pretty brunette girl in a bright yellow sundress and a couple boys dressed in shorts and golf shirts walked up to the group. "Hi, Amie! How's it going?" the girl smiled and gave Amie a hug.

"Pretty good, Hannah. Aren't you glad to be finished with sophomore year? I was definitely getting spring fever! How are you guys doing?"

"Good," the girl replied. "Amie, this is my boyfriend Evan and his brother, Drew."

"It's nice to meet you," said Amie. "Evan, I've heard good things about you. You're from Wenatchee, right?"

"Yes! We're here for the summer working at the drive-in. We're staying with Hannah's family."

"By the way, these are my housemates: Kendi, Hope, and Emma. They're all here in town to work summer season, too."

The girls exchanged pleasantries with Hannah, Evan, and Drew, and they talked for several minutes about their new jobs and summer plans.

Before long, it began to get dark, and Kendi yawned. "Sorry to be a party pooper, but I have an early shift tomorrow, so I'm going to head for home."

"Me, too," Hope nodded. "It was nice to meet all of you."

Hannah, Evan, and Drew left for home, too.

Just as Kendi and Hope were about to take off, they were surprised to see Ryan and Ben.

Ben was the first to speak. "Hey, Kendi! How was work today?" He smiled. "Sorry for abandoning you. My parents thought it would be easier to train the new girls if I wasn't there distracting you."

"I was wondering about that…" Kendi murmured.

"Kendi baked cookies today at work," Ryan stated.

"How do you know?" Ben asked.

"Oh, we hung out together this afternoon," Ryan revealed.

"Well, not exactly…" Kendi tried to say…

Before Kendi could finish speaking, Hope broke in: "We'd better get going."

"Yeah, I'll join you," Amie offered. "Coming, Emma?"

"Yes, that breeze is pretty cold." Emma shivered. "I should've worn a sweater."

"You're right. It gets pretty cool once the sun goes down. I'm definitely ready to get moving," Amie said. "See ya later, boys," she said in a cheerful voice.

"Will you be at the coffee shop tomorrow?" Emma asked Ben.

"You'll have to stop by and see," Ben responded with a wink.

Emma gave him a shy smile.

After several "See ya later" exchanges, the girls went off toward The Guesthouse, and the boys went towards the parking lot.

As the girls walked back, Emma pondered aloud whether Ben had a crush on her or was just flirty.

Amie warned her to pace herself. "You're going to meet a lot of boys this summer. Some are better than others, and it's best to just build friendships for now."

"I know you're right," Emma said "But I just need to remind myself of that … a lot!"

The other girls laughed.

"I think we are too young to commit to one person. I agree that friendships are best. What do you think, Hope?" Kendi said.

"I definitely won't get in a relationship," Hope said emphatically. "I don't want to lose sight of my goals."

"I'm weak in this area, so I'm glad that I'm with good roommates that'll help keep me strong." Emma sighed.

"Yeah, we'll keep you accountable," Amie said.

"Add me to the list," Kendi said. "I can be weak, too. It's sometimes nice to get positive attention from boys, but I know how quickly that can go south."

"I think we're all on the list," Amie laughed. "Let's steer clear from anything but group dates, and if any of us wants to pursue a relationship, let's agree to talk it through with the other 'Guesthouse Girls' first."

"Ha, I love our new name – 'Guesthouse Girls.' And I'll definitely stick to group dates only," Emma said with a nod as they approached their front door.

The girls piled into the house, and Aunty Nola greeted them. "Is everything okay?"

"Everything's fine. We were just having a talk about boys," Amie commented.

"Oh, yes. Every year, the summer workers come to town and sparks fly. I've seen it happen every year with the girls who stay here," Aunty Nola said knowingly. "Most of the time, it does not end well, unfortunately."

"I agree. We were just talking about how we all like the attention, but we decided that we should stick to going on group dates and not get serious with anyone, at least not for a while," Kendi reported.

"That is a probably a good idea," Aunty Nola said with approval. "It will give you a chance to get to know lots of people and not get tied into something until you are ready. I knew you were a wise group of girls!"

"Well, I guess it would be wise if we went to bed now," Emma giggled. "It's been a big day."

Each of the girls gave Aunty Nola a quick hug and headed up to bed. It was a little awkward for Hope because she did not do a lot of hugging, but Aunty Nola was so sweet and genuine that Hope felt drawn to her like a real aunt or grandma.

Each of the girls went to their own bedrooms. Emma and Kendi caught up on some texts, Amie read her daily devotional, and Hope called to check in with her mom.

It wasn't long before each girl was sound asleep.

CHAPTER SIX
First Tuesday

Hope spent some time thinking about what the girls discussed last night.

She had never been interested in dating back home, but she was surprised to find that she did enjoy Conner's flirting a little bit. However, she decided to run on a different trail today so she could avoid any meet-ups like yesterday.

Today, she was back to running alone, which was her comfort zone.

Afterwards she made it back to The Guesthouse, took a shower and dressed, then sat down and chatted with Aunty Nola before she had to leave for work.

"Have you talked to your mama lately?" Aunty Nola asked.

"Yes. We chatted last night a bit. She misses me," Hope said ruefully, "but she's getting lots of hours in at her weekend job, so she's happy about that."

"Do the two of you ever get a chance to go to church?" Nola asked.

"No…we've never really been church goers," Hope spoke, "but I really liked your church," she followed up quickly so as not to offend Aunty Nola.

"What did you like about it?"

"I liked the music. It wasn't old-fashioned and boring like I thought it would be. I also liked the talking part. The minister seemed really down-to-earth. I liked what he talked about…forgiveness."

"Yes, forgiveness is a great topic. I just finished teaching a class on that with the girls in my Bible study," Aunty Nola reflected.

"Oh, I would love to talk about that one morning," Hope remarked sincerely. "Maybe I could skip my run one day and we would have time to talk."

"I'd like that," Aunty Nola assured her.

"I'd better get moving now," Hope said while waving goodbye and set off for a work day on the beautiful shoreline.

◊ ◊◊◊ ◊

That evening, the girls gathered around the dinner table and recounted their day.

Hope talked about a boat fire she witnessed. "It wasn't one of my uncle's boats," Hope assured them, "but it was close to the shoreline where I work. The accident involved a man, a lady, two kids, and a little dog. We heard a loud popping sound, and then we saw flames shoot up out of the back of the boat. Uncle Joe told me to call 911, and then he jumped into one of our speedboats and drove out to the fire. He had a fire extinguisher, so he pulled up close to the other boat and was able to put out the flames. By then, the official rescue boat had arrived. They made sure that no one was injured first. Then, they tied a rope to the boat and towed them somewhere, probably to the boat dock where their car was parked," Hope speculated.

"Wow, that must've been scary!" Amie exclaimed.

"I'm sure it was for them. I was so relieved that no one was hurt. The whole incident lasted a few hours, including the report that my uncle had to give. I think it'll be on the news tonight," Hope added.

"Oh, we'll have to turn it on at 6 p.m. I wonder if it was a local family?" Aunty Nola mused.

"I'm not sure," Hope responded. "My uncle said he didn't recognize them. Anyway, how was your day, Amie?" she asked.

"It was really good. I've been enjoying working the front desk. The lady that has been training me has been hilarious. She tells me all kinds of funny stories about things that've happened at the hotel before, like demanding guests, mix ups with housekeeping, guests arriving on the wrong date, a visit from a prince of some small country, and everything in between. Most of the stories I've heard before, but it was fun to hear directly from someone who had a front row seat!"

"Wow, the visit from a prince must have been exciting," Emma chirped.

"Well, that story was funny. Someone from his country had called in advance to make the reservation, and they had a heavy accent. Whoever took the reservation put 'Prince' for the first name and the country for the last name because they thought that was the guy's name. When the prince arrived, he came with a huge staff and they thought that they were going to have the whole resort to themselves. Instead, they only had one room booked. You can imagine how upset they were because there were like 20 of them in the entourage," Amie shared.

"Were they able to be accommodated?" Aunty Nola questioned.

"No. It was high season, and they were lucky to even have one room," Amie continued. "However, they were very insistent, so my aunt and uncle were trying to figure out how to help them. They remembered that their friends, the Canberrys, who own several orchards, have a huge house on the water a few miles outside of town. They got a hold of them, and they happened to be out of town. They allowed the prince and his entourage to stay in their place. There was enough space for everybody because they used their pool house, too, plus a few of the buildings that are normally used for migrant workers. I guess everyone was happy eventually, and it all worked out. I heard that they left enormous tips for our cleaners who we sent to take care of them and some other staff. So, it started out bad, but it all ended up really good."

"What a great story!" the girls agreed.

"Oh, it looks like it is almost 6:00," Kendi realized. "Let's turn on the news and watch the story about the boat fire."

They turned on the local news channel, and the anchor covered a few stories about the town's preparation for the Memorial Day crowds. They then announced that after the break there was "some excitement on the water for one local family."

After the commercial, they could see the footage that a viewer had recorded with their phone. The video showed the boat in flames and Hope's Uncle Joe putting out the fire with his extinguisher. The reporter, Yvonne Getzen, who interviewed him after the rescue, called Joe a local hero for saving the family and their little dog. There was a small clip of her interview with Joe, a tanned and handsome blond man who looked a lot like Hope. He looked embarrassed from the attention and said that he was in the right place at the right time, and anyone would have done the same.

Yvonne Getzen also interviewed Hope and aired a little sound bite of her describing what she had observed as part of the story. The reporter closed with a statement: "Everyone would not have the presence of mind to act as quickly as Joe did, and we are lucky to have people like him in our town. After the commercial, we will be back to tell you some of the public events for Memorial Day weekend that you might want to add to your calendar."

With that, the newscast went to commercial, and the girls all clapped for Hope.

"We didn't know you would be on TV," Emma said proudly.

"It looks like you're a celebrity," Aunty Nola teased.

"Let's change the subject," Hope protested. "What did you do today, Emma?"

"I got to work at the ice cream counter in the back of the store," Emma began. "I sampled lots of flavors. It was really fun. I love that I'm getting cross-trained so I'll be able to help out wherever they need me. Oh," she changed subjects quickly, "I saw some of the people from the beach party in the store today. I saw Conner and Brett, and later, I saw Hannah and Evan. I also saw a family with a baby that I recognized from church. It's fun to actually know some people here already. Who did you see today, Kendi?" Emma inquired.

"Well, I was in the back room of the bakeshop most of the day, but later in the day, Ben and his brother Joseph came in. Ben worked for a few hours, and Joseph was returning some of the sound equipment they used at the beach party. The band is going to be playing at the Coffeeshop this weekend. They want to give people a clean alternative for some fun this weekend since the main street will be an alcohol fest."

"Yes," said Aunty Nola, "unfortunately, that happens on both the Memorial Day and Labor Day weekends. The town gets flooded with teenagers and young adults, and they cruise Main Street in their cars. Hundreds of kids walk up and down the sidewalks, and there is a lot of loud music and a lot of blatant drinking. There is always a big police presence, but they generally let the partying continue to run unless they must step in to break up fights. They also make sure nobody is bothering the businesses along Main Street.

We really wish they could shut it down, but it is kind of a tradition, and I just hope that nobody gets hurt, especially by a drunk driver," she added wistfully. "I'm so glad the coffee shop provides an alternative for young adults who don't want to be involved in the cruising scene."

"I agree, and Joseph's band is great. They play lots of genres of music. I'm excited for the weekend," Kendi said. "I'm actually going to be working, but I'll still be there to hear the music and see people. I'm training at the espresso counter tomorrow," she reported excitedly.

Emma's eyes sparkled. "It's going to be so fun!"

Amie looked out the window. "It looks like we missed sunset tonight," Amie remarked. "I need to stop by the resort because I forgot to give the kitchen some keys I had borrowed. Does anyone want to come with me?"

Kendi and Hope begged off, but Emma wanted to come. "Could you give me a tour?" she asked.

"Sure!" Amie said. "I love giving tours of the resort."

◊ ◊◊◊ ◊

Soon, the two girls were walking toward the resort.

"Amie, do you think it's bad to have a boyfriend?" Emma asked sincerely.

Amie answered thoughtfully. "I definitely don't believe in casual dating, but I think if a couple is committed to making good choices, then maybe."

"I was wondering cause I've never had a boyfriend, and I was hoping to get one soon," Emma confessed.

"Well, I wouldn't rush into anything. I think it's better to start off as friends and get to know the boy. Every summer, there are boys and girls getting drunk and hooking up. It probably happens that way everywhere, but it definitely happens in this town. There are often unintended consequences that sometimes include pregnancies, disease, and broken hearts," Amie said decisively. I personally know two girls who got pregnant from summer flings last year and one of them was just a freshman who hooked up with an older guy whose parents have a summer home here. He had no interest in her, besides the obvious, and when he found out she was pregnant, he told her to get an abortion. She refused and now she moved into her grandma's house and her grandma watches the baby when she is in school. Her parents are not supportive at all and they didn't want the baby in their house. Based on that, I'm sure that girl would advise you to not rush into any relationship this summer.

"I know, and I agree...but I just want someone to hang out with and hold hands with. I want someone to tell me I'm pretty. I feel stupid saying this," Emma said.

"It's okay, Emma. I'm sure most people feel that way. I feel like God created us with a desire to be with someone. I just don't think we should jump into a relationship until we are reasonably sure that it is someone who we could see a future with. It's important that we think with our head as well as our heart. I don't think guys our age do that very often so we can't count on them to protect us in that way."

Just as they were finishing their discussion, the girls arrived at the resort. "Now, are you ready for a tour?" Amie asked with a smile.

"Absolutely!" Emma said. "My family and I have never stayed here before, and I've really wanted to see it."

"Okay! Well, let's start with the restaurant. I need to drop off some keys."

They climbed the stairs on the outside of the building. When they got to the reception desk for the restaurant, they were greeted by a smiling young blond man whose face lit up when he saw the girls.

"Hi Josh!" Amie greeted him with a grin. "I haven't seen you all week!"

"I know! They must be keeping you busy. We've been working hard getting the restaurant and lunch counter ready for high season and training the summer staff. By the way, my name's Josh," he said with a smile, extending his hand to Emma.

"Nice to meet you. I'm Emma," she said, accepting his handshake. "I'm staying at The Guesthouse with Amie this summer and working at the general store."

"Oh, that'll be fun! Mr. Femley is really nice."

Just then, a couple came in with a reservation and Josh grabbed some shiny red menus and turned his attention to them.

"Nice to see you girls," he said over his shoulder. "Amie, you should stop by on your lunch break sometime and we can catch up in between customers, if it's not too busy."

"Will do," she called back to him as she and Emma turned to leave.

"Hey Josh," Amie got his attention, "catch!"

"What are these?" he asked reaching a hand up and snatching the object from the air.

"Keys to the storage room! I forgot and took them home with me."

He smiled. "Okay! thanks!"

"So, back to the tour," Amie continued as she walked down the hall and around a corner. "Stillwaters is our fancier restaurant, and this is our casual lunch counter called Beaches. People sitting out by one of the pools or beach area can order, and our staff can bring their lunch out to them."

"There's more than one pool?" Emma asked excitedly.

"Yes, actually! There are four. One is for adults only, one is more of a kiddie pool area, and the other two are just normal pools," Amie explained.

"Can we see them?" Emma asked.

"Of course," Amie answered as they walked down the steps to get to the lobby. "Here is the reservation desk where I am working this summer. I'm learning the system because we're going to have a zillion guests checking in this weekend, and we'll likely be completely booked all summer. I'll show you one of the empty rooms, and then we can check out one of the pools. We only keep one of the pools open after dark, and it has tiki torches that we light at night. Lots of people hang out at the pool area and watch the sunset."

They reached the front desk and were greeted by a smiling woman who looked around the age of 50. "Hi Linda, are there any rooms available that I can show Emma?"

"Sure! 112 is open until tomorrow afternoon," Lynn suggested.

"Perfect! See you tomorrow!" Amie said as she waved cheerfully.

The girls walked down the resort path until they came to one of the rooms. Amie unlocked it with her master key card.

Emma walked in and caught her breath. "This room is so beautiful… and look at that view! Are they all like this?" Emma breathed.

Amie laughed. "No, this is one of the VIP suites. The rest of the rooms are nice, but not this elegant and not as panoramic of a view. Follow me, we can check out the pool and head for home."

They walked out of the hotel room and down to the beautiful pool area and saw several people enjoying drinks poolside under the soft lighting of the moon and the tiki torches. They looked farther across the lawn and saw a group gathered around a fire pit singing songs played by a boy with a guitar.

"Wow, this is a cool place. I hope I can stay here someday," Emma gushed.

Amie laughed. "Me, too. I've never actually stayed here as a guest. We had to stay here one time when a pipe broke at our house, but it wasn't in the summer, and it was cold and miserable and pouring down rain.

The pools weren't open, and it was pretty lame. However, sometime, I'll definitely stay here in a different capacity!" Amie looked down at her watch and gasped when she saw the time. "We'd better get home, now."

The two girls hurried home, went to their own bedrooms, and slept well after their walk in the late spring air.

CHAPTER SEVEN
Friday Night Fun

The next couple of days passed by uneventfully for the girls, except for chance meetings with new friends at their various workplaces.

As predicted, the town started to fill with visitors. By Friday, the one road that entered town from the west was slowed to a crawl with bumper-to-bumper traffic for over a mile.

Kendi had enjoyed her time on Wednesday and Thursday learning the coffee shop operations. On Friday, she was given a late shift so she could help serve coffee with Ben during the special music event, and she was very excited about it. She arrived at 4 o' clock that afternoon and waved to Reed, who had just finished her shift and was leaving for the day. Reed told Kendi that she was thinking of stopping by later to see the music, but she might not want to battle traffic coming back into town.

Kendi started her shift by making sure that all the cups, lids, and stirrers were stocked and that the hopper was full of whole beans to be freshly ground as needed. She cleaned the area, then went back to the walk-in refrigerator to get more milk and cream to put in the cooler behind the front counter.

Now, bring on the crowds, she thought to herself proudly *I'm ready!*

Just then, Ben sauntered through the front door.

"You're late," Kendi teased cheerfully.

"I just wanted to make sure you had all the work done behind the counter before I got here," he explained.

"What?" Kendi said with her eyes wide with feigned exasperation in her voice. She was just kidding, because nothing could dampen her enthusiasm tonight.

"No, I actually had to run into town today to pick up some new speakers. Joseph's going to be here any minute to get them set up."

"Are you excited, or is this just status quo for you?" Kendi asked.

"Oh no, I get excited every time we do a special event. I love live music, and I love to see all the people." he added. "By the way, are your housemates coming?"

"Yes! Amie and Emma wouldn't miss it, and they'll talk Hope into coming…although I'm sure she would rather be working out or going on a run."

"Don't you like her?" Ben asked.

"No, I totally love Hope. But she would tell you herself that crowds aren't her thing. Amie will stick with her, and they can leave if it got too crowded."

Joseph arrived a little later, and Kendi and Ben

busied themselves setting up the chairs and tables so everyone who arrived could have a view of the stage area. Ben showed Kendi where extra chairs were stored in case the crowd was bigger than they expected.

Earlier today, Rachel had prepared both sweet and savory treats because she knew some people would want dinner-type foods. She had some mini quiches and pot pies for people to buy besides her brownies, cookies, and other treats. Ben said she usually came close to selling out of her baked goods on nights like these. Rachel would be manning the pastry counter and Kendi, Ben, and his dad Mark would be serving the drinks.

The concert didn't start until 7 o' clock, but people started arriving at 6. It was non-stop busy behind the coffee counter for the next four hours.

Kendi had the time of her life making and serving hot and iced coffee drinks. She saw her housemates come in but barely had time for more than a quick hello. She also saw lots of people she had met at the beach party and at the sunset on Monday night. At one point, she looked up and saw a good-looking blond boy who looked a lot like Amie sitting at the table with Amie, Emma, and Hope. A while later, she noticed that Brett and Conner had joined them.

The music is perfect, and the vibe here is amazing, Emma thought as she hung out at the table with Amie and Hope. Emma had been a bit worried that she would rather be out on the lively street with all the partiers. She knew that kids out there cruising had a lot of fun, and she was worried that it might be a little lame in the coffee shop. However, she was pleasantly surprised; the action was nonstop, and the girls had opportunities to talk to many of their new friends, even though they could barely hear themselves over the music.

Emma was so glad she had made the decision to come to Chelan this summer. She was becoming part of a group that she had always dreamed of. The high school she went to in Pasco was huge. Although she had friends in her school clubs, it was very easy to get lost in the crowd, and she didn't have many close friends.

The church that her family attended on Christmas and Easter back home was pretty old-fashioned, and there weren't a lot of kids there to hang out with, even if her family went there all the time. Everyone in this new group in Chelan either went to Amie's church, or they were friends with someone who did. She knew that no one in this group was going to be perfect, but at least she was finding good friends.

Maybe I'll even find a boyfriend, Emma thought with a smile while scanning the room.

Hope hadn't wanted to come, but the girls talked her into stopping by for a while. After they'd arrived, she decided she was glad she came. Brett and Conner had stopped by their table, and she was perfectly comfortable hanging out with them in this setting because there were lots of other people milling around. She was definitely not interested in dating anyone at this point, although it seemed like Conner was interested in her, and Brett might be as well. She enjoyed the music and atmosphere and had a surprisingly good time.

Amie was surprised to see Josh show up at the coffee shop, probably because she had mainly seen him only at work. She motioned for him to sit down with her and her roommates, and she was surprised that she felt a little nervous. His smile was so infectious, and she realized that she might be developing a slight crush on him. She laughed at herself and decided that was crazy.

At 11 o' clock, the band ended their set, and the last hour was reserved for karaoke. Kendi half-wished that she could put her name on the list to sing, but she knew that they were too busy, and it probably wasn't appropriate since she was working. Pretty soon she heard from the microphone that the next song was "Summer Loving" from *Grease*. She was not surprised because that was a popular Karaoke duet.

She *was* surprised to hear her name being called to come to the stage and sing it with Ryan.

Whaaat? I didn't sign up for this. I'm working. I've never practiced this song and certainly not with Ryan.

Before she had time to think any more, Mark and Ben were pushing her in the direction of the stage. The coffee shop was still full, although not as crowded as it was earlier, and people weren't really ordering coffee.

She reached the stage and picked up her microphone. She gave Ryan a grin that said, *I'm going to get you for this*, and they proceeded to perform an animated version of this crowd favorite.

When they finished, Rachel gave her a high five and asked her if she knew Ryan had put their names in for the karaoke contest.

Kendi said, "I had no idea!"

"Well, you sounded great anyway." Rachel gushed. "We'll definitely have to get you on stage more this summer."

Kendi received lots of compliments from both her friends, as well as strangers, as the crowd trickled out for the evening.

By midnight, they had mostly cleaned up behind the counter. Ben and his dad were going to stick around a while to sell coffee to some of the late-night crowd of cruisers who invariably came around to get coffee after their partying. Mark had explained earlier that if the coffee could draw them in, he could use the time to get in conversations with them. Mark liked to talk to people about God in a non-threatening way, and the coffee shop gave him lots of opportunities to do so.

Mark looked at Rachel and asked, "Honey, do you want to take Kendi home? She's already worked a full shift and it's going to be another late night tomorrow."

"Absolutely! I'll drop Kendi off and go home and get some beauty sleep. You and Ben can come home together later in Ben's car," Rachel replied, relieved that she could finally go home.

As they walked to Rachel's car, Rachel asked Kendi how the night went for her.

"It was amazing. I feel like I'm living my dream right now," Kendi said.

"Do you miss your parents and friends?" Rachel asked.

"Well, we call and text a lot, so it's like I never left," she explained.

"I'm glad you're having fun, and I'm also glad that you get to stay with Aunty Nola. She is a wise woman, and you will learn a lot from her."

"I'm sure I will," Kendi agreed. "Thank you for the ride! I'll see you tomorrow at 4 o' clock!"

Kendi shut the front door behind her and saw the light go out in Aunty Nola's room. She smiled knowing that Aunty Nola waited for all the girls to get home before falling asleep. She was happy that Aunty Nola gave them the freedom to do their own thing, but also provided a safety net for them. She never wanted to abuse Aunty Nola's trust.

With that, she went to her room and quickly fell asleep.

Judy Ann Koglin

CHAPTER EIGHT
Saturday Shenanigans

Hope woke up bright and early and headed to Joe's Jet Skis and Boat Rentals. She knew it would be crazy-busy today, and she wanted to get everything in order before the phone started ringing.

Joe was already there and had checked out their three fishing boats to eager fishermen. The families who rented the four pontoon boats had already checked them out for the weekend yesterday. In a little while, there would be a family who was renting a speed boat for the day, and all day long, there would be people coming in every hour to rent the Jet Skis and WaveRunners. She would have to have them sign liability waivers and pay for the rentals, while some of Joe's other employees would get them set up with life jackets and take them to their watercraft.

She spread sunscreen on her skin that was already becoming tan from being out in the sun so much this week. Earlier this week, when it was slow, she and Uncle Joe got to take a couple of jet skis out for a spin.

Hope loved how freeing it felt to whiz around the lake with her hair blowing behind her and the wind in her face. She felt so empowered as she raced across the fairly empty lake. This had to be the best feeling in the world, and she could see exactly why Uncle Joe chose this line of work.

Her reminiscing was interrupted by her first phone call of the day. "Joe's Jet Skis, this is Hope," she answered.

"Hi, how much to rent a jet ski?" the caller asked.

Hope recited the pricing, then explained that they were booked solid today, but had an opening tomorrow at 2 o' clock.

After some back-and-forth conversation, the caller took that reservation. Once that call was completed, Sunday was fully booked, except for the occasional expected cancellation. Joe's policy was to always take a 50% non-refundable deposit on the phone so people would think twice about canceling. It was a lesson Uncle Joe had learned the hard way to prevent no-shows. He had experienced one too many cancellations at the last minute back when each dollar could be the difference between being able to pay his bills or losing his hard-earned business. The implementation of the non-refundable deposit was a big part of the reason he was able to thrive while running a business that received the vast majority of its income from the last week of May through the first week of September.

Over at Mr. Femley's General Store, Emma was just unlocking the front glass door from the inside and turning the light blue sign to the Open position. The sun was shining through the window, and that always put Emma in a good mood.

Emma was excited because she was just working a short shift today and was going to lie in the sun with Kendi after work before Kendi had to leave for her late shift at the coffee shop. Emma and the other "Guesthouse Girls" would head over there later to listen to the band and mingle with other teenagers. Emma smiled, anticipating another fun night.

She was on register duty today and was assigned to Register 1. She liked that one the best because she was too short to see who walked through the door when she was working at Registers 2 and 3. This way, she got to see everyone who entered, and boy, did they enter! All day long, in fact. And now, it was not only the locals coming through the doors, but also tourist families looking to replace a wayward swimsuit or bottle of sunscreen that they had forgotten to pack.

Emma soon realized that Register 1 might not be the best spot for the new girl because she was interrupted during each transaction by people demanding to know where a certain item was located, and she would get flustered and lose her place with the customer she was ringing up.

After a few mistakes, Emma told Mr. Femley that she might need to go to Register 2 or 3 because she was so distracted. She felt terrible having to admit it, though.

"Emma, I am proud of you for telling me that," Mr. Femley replied reassuringly. "There is no shame in needing a better atmosphere to concentrate on your customer. Let's move you to 2 for now and we'll see if that is less distracting."

That move worked like a charm, and Emma spent the next few hours working the register like a pro.

It wasn't long before Tricia sent her on her break. Emma wasted no time rushing over to her favorite coffee shop for a drink. She knew Kendi wasn't working right now, but she hoped she would catch a glimpse of Ben. She got her wish because, although his shift didn't start until later that day, he was borrowing his dad's truck so he could use it to take his kayak to the dock for an afternoon paddle.

"Hi, Emma!" he called cheerfully. "I didn't expect to see you here."

She grabbed her iced mocha from the counter and said thank you to the friendly barista, whose name tag said Reed. She turned her attention to Ben. "I didn't think you would be here either," Emma stammered. "I mean, I thought you would be working later tonight," she tried to explain.

"I am working later tonight. I'm just grabbing the truck so I can go kayaking with my friend. Have you ever kayaked before?" he inquired.

"Not with a boy—I mean, not lately," she corrected herself quickly. "I went with my family a few times."

"Well, maybe we can take a spin around the lake sometime?" Ben offered.

"Um, that would be fun. No, I can't. Maybe I can," she said in rapid-fire succession as she was trying to figure out if this would be as friends, as a date, or possibly with a group, or just a polite offer that he didn't really mean.

"Emma, I can't figure you out sometimes. You are so funny." Ben said, perplexed. Seeing her face fall in disappointment, he added "and cute."

Emma's face reddened. "I gotta go, my break's over! See ya tonight!" she cried over her shoulder as she sprinted back to Mr. Femley's General Store, clutching her drink. Her ice cubes added percussion to her short run back to work as they jostled around in the cold brown liquid.

Ben's comment about her being cute lifted her spirits even more than the iced mocha did, and the rest of her shift flew by as she busily helped customer after customer.

At 1 o' clock sharp, Emma pushed her paper time card into the vintage time clock and punched out for the day. She ran home as quickly as she could so she could maximize her sun tanning time with Kendi.

When she got home, she greeted Aunty Nola hurriedly on her way up the stairs to put on her blue bikini and coordinating cover-up. Kendi was ready and had two plush beach towels along with some coconut-scented suntan lotion and two water bottles packed in a cute beach bag with a beach umbrella stenciled on it that she had purchased last time her family was on a trip.

The two girls flew down the stairs and out the door, yelling a hurried good-bye to Aunty Nola, who was already aware of their plans.

"Don't get sunburned, girls!" Aunty Nola called after them with a smile and a shake of her head.

◊ ◊◊◊ ◊

The two girls headed to the public boat docks. On the way there, they stopped by to see Hope at Joe's Jetskis.

"Hey, beautiful!" Kendi said as they found Hope, who had just finished up doing the paperwork with a couple of guys renting watercraft.

"Oh, hi! What are you doing here?" Hope asked, surprised to see her roommates. "Wait, I remember, you were going to catch some rays this afternoon. Let me introduce you guys to my uncle really quick." She motioned for him to come over. "Uncle Joe, these are two of my roommates, Kendi and Emma."

The girls exchanged "nice to meet yous" with Uncle Joe and Kendi asked Hope if she was coming to the coffee shop later.

"Wouldn't miss it," she said with enthusiasm.

After saying goodbye to Hope, Kendi and Emma cheerfully chatted as they walked the rest of the way to the boat docks, spread out their towels, and applied their new coconut sunscreen. The girls laughed about how Hope had to be dragged to the coffee shop last night but was excited to come today. They shrugged, reclined on their towels, and closed their eyes under their shades and chatted as the sun warmed their skin.

Pretty soon after they initially laid out, they both dozed off to sleep for a few minutes before they were awakened by a male voice saying, "fancy meeting you two here."

They looked up and saw Ben standing near them holding two paddles as his friend Cody, a lanky boy with brown hair and eyes whom Kendi had met at the beach party, pulled a kayak from the water.

The girls laughed. "We aren't following you, we promise," they insisted.

"Well, a guy can dream, right?" Ben joked. They talked for a moment, and then Ben remembered what time it was. "Hey, I need to hustle because we need to get this kayak out of the water, get Cody back home, and get the truck back to my dad within an hour. See you girls later!" He and Cody waved at the girls as they carried the kayak up to the parking lot to load it in the back of the truck.

◊ ◊◊◊ ◊

"Cute girls," Cody remarked. "I remember the ginger from the beach party,"

"Yes, that is Kendi, and she works at the coffee shop. The one with the curly hair is her roommate Emma."

"You always know all the girls," Cody pouted.

"I know; I kinda do. But knowing them hasn't gotten me far, as you may have noticed," Ben replied ruefully.

"Ya, I *have* noticed that. You're in the same boat as me." Cody laughed at his unintentional pun as the two of them carried the kayak to the truck.

"Maybe this is our year," Ben grinned. The boys finished securing the kayak in the back of the truck and hopped into the cab.

"I'd settle for a date or two," Cody smirked, as they buckled their seatbelts and drove away.

◊ ◊◊◊ ◊

Meanwhile, Emma was sharing her worries with Kendi that Ben was going to think she orchestrated their sunbathing session just to see him since he had mentioned going kayaking earlier.

"Not a chance, Emma," Kendi reassured her friend. "There are tons of places that he could have put his boat in, and it was a coincidence that it was at the same place where we were. If I have a chance, I will make that clear tonight."

"Oh, that'll be good. Thanks, Kendi. By the way, I know we have agreed only to do group dates for a while this summer, but tell me the truth: do you think you and Ben might be interested in each other?" Emma asked earnestly. "I don't want to break the girl code if you like each other, and I suppose you have dibs because you work together."

Kendi laughed. "Emma, I didn't come to Chelan looking for a boyfriend. I came here to sing, make coffee for people, and earn some spending money. As for Ben, I'm not sure how I feel about him. He is good-looking, I can't deny that, and he is friendly, but not just with me. I think it's just his way, so I can't say if he has feelings for me. But, what I can assure you is that I don't have 'dibs' on him. If you two find that you are interested in each other, I absolutely will not stand in your way. You definitely would be a great looking couple with your beautiful skin and hair and petite little body and his tall blond handsomeness. Let's just take it slow and see how things play out this summer."

"Ok," Emma agreed reluctantly. "How much longer before you need to go to get ready for work?"

Kendi consulted her phone, "we should probably go back in about 45 minutes."

The girls closed their eyes, relaxed, and soon fell asleep again under a gentle breeze.

About 40 minutes later, Kendi jolted awake, unsure of how long she had slept. She looked at her phone for the time. "Emma, wake up! We fell asleep again. I was freaking out because I thought we had slept too long, but we are right on time if we leave now."

Emma opened her eyes and rubbed them, feeling a little drowsy after her nap in the sunshine. "Yeah, we'd better go before we get sunburned anyway," Emma pointed out.

The girls walked home. Kendi took a cool shower because she was still really warm from all the sun and got dressed for work. She was excited to start her shift. She had been honest with Emma in that she didn't know how she felt about Ben, and she didn't know how he felt about her either. She did know she always hoped that he would be working on her shift because he made things really fun. However, Kendi really did believe that Ben and Emma would be a cute couple, and she had to consider the possibility that Ben liked Emma as much as Emma appeared to like him.

"Oh, well. Not my problem right now," Kendi murmured to herself as she hurried to work, and her freshly-combed damp hair dried in the sun.

CHAPTER NINE
Saturday Night Music

Just like déjà vu, Emma, Amie, and Hope got ready for the coffee shop concert...but something was different tonight. There was less nervousness, especially on Hope's part, because they knew what to expect.

Hope tended to be a loner at home, mainly by her own choice. She played sports and had friends that were teammates, but her family did not have the money that the rest of the girls seemed to have, so she tended to withdraw from people so she wouldn't be disappointed when they went places and she didn't have the money to join in. Her mom knew this was the case and worried about her, and she hoped that The Guesthouse experience that her brother Joe had offered to fund would be a chance for Hope to make some real friends.

Hope was surprised to find that she was actually excited to go tonight and that the girls did not have to coax her. She brushed out her hair and even put on a little makeup from Amie's vast makeup collection.

The girls had already gotten in the habit of borrowing each other's clothes when offered. They all could wear a size small, but they all had different body styles. Hope was the tallest of the four girls and very lean, like a model. Amie was the tiniest with a small bone structure. She actually fit just as well in large kid-sized clothing. Emma was small like Amie, but much curvier with an hourglass figure. Kendi was taller than Amie and Emma, but not as tall as Hope. She was actually pretty athletic in frame and always got an easy A in P.E. class, but she didn't play organized sports. She much preferred playing music, had recently auditioned for a before-school select choir, and was also part of an after-school jazz choir.

The girls headed to the coffee shop a little early so they could commandeer two tables and push them together so they could accommodate their friends who would likely show up, based on how well last night went.

The three girls went up to the counter and ordered drinks. Kendi took their orders, wrote their names and drink selections on their cups, and passed the cup on to Mark Brandon. Hope got a raspberry iced tea, Emma went for an iced mocha, and Amie ordered an iced caramel latte.

Hope sat down to save their places, and Emma and Amie waited patiently near the counter for their drinks, chatting about the types of music that they liked to listen to and which songs they hoped the band would play tonight.

Before long, they heard Ben call their names, and they retrieved their drinks from him.

He smiled at them and said, "Back for more, huh?"

Amie teased, "Yeah, it was either this or stay home and go to bed early, so this sounded like a better option."

Ben responded, "You'll be glad you came. Joseph's going to talk at intermission tonight. Say a quick prayer for him that people will listen to what he has to say?"

"Will do," Amie said, and Emma nodded in agreement.

When they walked back to their seats, Emma asked Amie, "Is Ben religious?"

Amie seemed taken aback by the question. "Well, I wouldn't say 'religious.' He's a Christian, like me."

"Oh, I'm Christian, too," Emma said. "My family goes to church a few times each year but I don't really know much about what they talk about there."

Amie made a mental note to talk more about this with Emma later. She was pretty sure that Emma thought that attending a Christian church occasionally made you a Christian.

They were interrupted by a sound check. By then, the place started filling up with people, and it soon became too noisy to continue their conversation.

The band started out with "Sweet Home Alabama," which got the whole place singing, and then followed that up with hits through the decades.

The girls had so much fun that the time passed quickly.

At one point, the band took a break, and Joseph took the mic, quieting the chatting.

"Hey, guys!" he addressed the crowd. "On behalf of everyone here at Brandon's Coffee and Bakeshop, and the band, I wanted to thank you guys for coming out and supporting us. We'll be back to playing in just a few minutes. I just wanted to take a minute to tell you a little about our band. We started this group when we were still in high school, and we got our start in my parents' rec room. We started playing here at the coffee shop, and then we got chances to play at church events and even a few weddings. Then, we started booking company picnics and bigger events in Wenatchee. At this point, our calendar is really full, on top of us finishing up our college degrees this year!"

At that, the crowd broke into applause and cheers, and the band nodded their appreciation.

"Thank you so much," Joseph continued. "On the drums, we have Aiden, who majored in political science and public policy. On bass is Logan, who is majoring in Chemistry. On keyboards is Noah, who majored in performing arts, and I'm Joseph. I'm the lead singer and can pick up an instrument or two from time to time, but these guys are better. I majored in Biblical Studies. I figured because of my major, I would be remiss if I didn't invite you to come check out our church tomorrow morning. It starts early at 9 –I know, I know it's early for us too–but then we have all day to wakeboard or just enjoy the sun afterward. At our church, we sing and learn something from God's Word.

It's not a place of judgment, but a place of love, and I encourage you to check it out tomorrow. If you aren't sure about church but just have questions about a God who loves you no matter what you've done, feel free to hit one of us up after the show ends tonight. Thanks for listening. Now, go buy a latte or a pastry, and we will be back with more songs in five minutes." With that, he turned music on through the house sound system.

The lines at the two registers got really long, but Kendi and the rest of the crew did a great job getting orders processed quickly.

Amie caught Joseph's eye and mouthed the words, "Great job!" to which he nodded his appreciation.

Emma went up to the counter and bought a bottle of water and a cookie for herself. When she got to the front of the line, she was meaning to ask Kendi how she was holding up, but she didn't have to ask. Kendi was radiant. She was definitely in her element in the coffee shop, especially when there was live music and a crowd to serve. It was fun to see.

Emma had a fleeting assumption that maybe Kendi's glow was because she got to work in close proximity to Ben, but she let the thought go.

There were still lines when the band came up and resumed playing crowd favorites. After another hour, Joseph told the crowd that they were going to sing one more song in honor of Memorial Day Weekend, and then they would change to karaoke for the last hour.

Ben turned to Kendi as they were cleaning up the espresso area, "Hey, do you want to do a duet tonight?

I thought I should ask before Ryan ambushes you and makes you sing a Grease song again!"

"Sure! Do you want to do the duet from Aladdin?" Kendi asked.

"I can show you the world," Ben sung back to her. "I'll put it in the queue for us."

The band started their final song, "God Bless the USA," and the whole coffee shop sung the choruses together.

"That was a perfect way to end the concert," Hope remarked to Emma and the others at their table.

"We can't leave yet," Emma implored. "Ben and Kendi are going to sing a duet."

"Okay, well, hopefully they will be first, because I'm beat!" Hope sighed ruefully.

The first few singers were really good, and they were followed by a couple who weren't as talented, but had a lot of enthusiasm.

Then, it was Kendi and Ben's turn. They did a great job singing "A Whole New World," and when they were finished, the girls congratulated them. Amie told Kendi that the girls were going to head home.

Kendi thanked them for coming and told them that she would catch a ride back when she was done working.

The cleanup process was already finished before the karaoke hour was finished. Mark told Ben and Kendi that they were free to go, and that Ben could drop her off. Kendi was glad because she was tired, and she didn't mind a chance to ride with Ben.

She told Ben that she wished that she would have gotten her license this spring when she turned 16, so she could drive herself around this summer and not have to be a bother.

"You're no trouble," Ben laughed. "It is kind of like having a little sister who hasn't turned 16 yet."

"But I *have* turned 16, and I am *not* your sister."

"I know, I was just joking." Changing the subject, he said, "You're a great singer, Kendi. Have you had formal training?"

"Well, I've been in choirs and choruses all my life, and I've learned a lot from my music teachers."

"Do you get to sing a lot at your church in Redmond?"

"To be honest, I don't even go to church," Kendi admitted. "We used to go when I was younger, and I liked it, but as I got older, our family has gotten busier, and we went less often, and now don't go at all. I always hear that kids on American Idol and The Voice got their start at church, so I wished that we went to church so I could gain that type of singing experience." Kendi said wistfully.

Ben looked a little taken aback by her comment, and Kendi couldn't figure out why. He slowly responded, "Well, I'm glad you have a church to attend this summer, then."

"Me, too," Kendi said, still really confused by his reaction. She tried to think of what she had said that would have caused Bento shut down so quickly, and what she could say to fix it.

To her disappointment, she couldn't think of anything to say, and the remainder of the short car ride was spent in awkward silence. Kendi had originally hoped this drive would be time to get clarification about how Ben felt, but decided quickly that this was not the time to delve into that.

They reached The Guesthouse. Ben said goodbye and dropped her off, just as his mom had done the previous night.

CHAPTER TEN
A Special Sunday

The next morning, Aunty Nola and "The Guesthouse Girls" got ready for church. They walked together quietly because they were all tired from their busy week. Even bubbly Emma, who was rarely quiet, plodded along in silence.

Aunty Nola and Hope were having a quiet conversation as they walked a few paces ahead of the other three girls. They had grown quite close over their morning talks. Hope was strangely drawn to Aunty Nola, as if she was really her aunt or grandma. Hope's family was really small with just her mom and Uncle Joe, so being in The Guesthouse had been a nice change.

Soon, they arrived at church and sat close to where they had sat the previous week. The girls looked around and found that they recognized many more faces this Sunday because of people they had met both at their various jobs and at the weekend concerts. They waved to their new friends and felt much more at home this week.

Ben was sitting a few rows ahead of them with his family, and he waved back at the girls. "Talk to me afterwards," he mouthed silently toward them.

The pastor spoke about sacrifice this week, tying his sermon into Memorial Day, when many brave soldiers had sacrificed their lives over the years, and their loved ones had sacrificed their husbands and children who were in the military for the good of the country. He asked people to raise their hand if they lost someone who was killed during any of the military conflicts. Many of the older people raised their hands, including Aunty Nola, and some of the younger people did as well.

The pastor thanked them sincerely for their sacrifice of the loved one. "If you were a spouse or parent of someone who lost their life, you made a huge sacrifice of your time with this person because they chose to go defend our country. Thank you for this sacrifice. For the people who lost their lives, they made the ultimate sacrifice to give their lives for others. It is hard to imagine such selfless service. These individuals didn't even know most of you; in fact, many of you had not even been born yet. But they made the sacrifice to serve their country and die for your freedom. It is pretty staggering if you think about it.

"However," the pastor continued, "there is someone else who made a choice to sacrifice Himself for you and a Father who allowed His Son to make that sacrifice. That person is Jesus, God's Son, who left the comforts of Heaven to come to earth and become a carpenter's son.

He lived a perfect life. Let that sink in. *A. Perfect. Life.*
No sin. No lies. No disobedience to his parents. *No. Bad.*
Thoughts. Absolute perfection. He was the Son of God,
and the Bible tells us that He *was* God, part of the three
in one Godhead–The Father, The Son, and The Holy
Spirit.

"Then, there's you," the pastor said with a lopsided
grin, and the people in the crowd laughed nervously.
"It may surprise you, but God knew you before you
were even born. In Jeremiah 1:5 it reads, *"Before I formed*
thee in the belly, I knew thee…" He knew everything you
would ever do, all the sins you would ever commit, all
your shortcomings, your insecurities, and your secrets.
But with full knowledge of how sinful every one of us
is, He chose to send Jesus. Indeed, Jesus chose to come
and sacrifice Himself so that you personally could have
a relationship with the one true God. Isaiah 53:5 says
that, *"He was wounded for our transgressions…"* He loved
you that much. Jesus came to earth, lived a perfect life,
healed people, fed people, gave people hope, and
ultimately allowed them to nail Him to a cross in the
ultimate sacrifice. He knew that without this sacrifice,
the sin in our life would prevent us from having a
relationship with God, who is holy. We needed to get
rid of our sin, and Jesus Christ's sacrifice and
resurrection allowed us to do just that. He can cleanse
your sins, even now, over 2000 years later. If you accept
this free gift that He is offering, Jesus will forgive your
sins, and give you access to a relationship with His
Father which will allow you to go to Heaven someday.

The Bible tells us in Romans 6:23, *"For the wages of sin is death but the gift of God is eternal life through Christ Jesus our Lord."*

The girls had been looking around during this sermon and had seen various people, including Aunty Nola and Amie, nodding at various parts of the talk. They even heard a few people saying "Amen" softly after different points. Kendi remembered back to when she was little and went to Sunday school a lot, and she knew she had heard something like this before. It made a lot of sense.

The pastor asked, "Is there any reason why you wouldn't want to accept a gift of this magnitude? I guarantee it is the greatest gift you could ever get. Sometimes, people don't accept this gift because they don't feel like they are good enough. I assure you–you are not good enough–and neither am I. But God is good enough, and He has deemed you worthy. That is why you are here today. In a minute, I am going to have everyone close their eyes, and I am going to pray. If you want to accept this gift, please pray silently after me as I lead you in a prayer. If you are sincere, He will come into your life and forgive your sins, you will be saved, and this will be a new beginning for you."

The pastor led the group in prayer, and Kendi realized that this was something that she wanted. The pastor made some good points, but she was really convinced because of what she felt inside her. It was amazing. It was as if God Himself was telling her how much she was loved, and she was ready to receive it.

When it was time, she decided to pray along with the pastor and accept the sacrifice Jesus had made for her.

After the prayer was over, Kendi had a remarkable sense of peace. She couldn't wait to tell Aunty Nola what she had done.

After church, there was some social time, and Aunty Nola was busy with people coming up to her for a hug or a conversation. Kendi wandered slowly out to the lobby to join the girls.

They had gone over to the coffee makers situated on tables to get some coffee, and she saw Ben walking toward her.

"Hi, Kendi," he greeted her with a big grin. "I wanted to tell you girls something–"

"Oh, wait! I want to tell you something too!" Kendi interrupted. "I prayed the prayer with the pastor today. I'm so happy! I finally get it."

Ben gave her a huge smile and a side hug and said, "I am so happy for you, Kendi! Welcome to the family!"

Just then, the girls returned with their coffees. Kendi told them what she had done.

Amie reacted the same way Ben had, wearing a grin and giving her a hug. "I'm so excited for you!" Amie cheered, her blue eyes sparkling. "You'll always remember this day. Do you have a Bible?"

"Not here," Kendi said.

"Don't worry, we'll get you one, and you can download the app, too," Amie assured her.

"Hey Ben, I interrupted you. What did you want to tell us?" Kendi asked him.

"Oh, I just wanted to tell you that Ryan wanted to invite all of us to a party at the water park on Sunday afternoon two weeks from now. They have it every year, and he was thinking about doing it today, but his parents thought Memorial Day weekend would be too crowded. So, if all of you can get off work that day, please do, because it'll be epic. After the park closes, we get to stay after and ride some of the slides with no lines. Then, we'll have a big bonfire, a dinner, and a devotional."

All the girls loved the idea and promised to see if they could get off work that Sunday.

Just then, Aunty Nola emerged with some of her friends in tow. Once everyone said their goodbyes, the girls and Aunty Nola headed for home.

Kendi told Aunty Nola her good news and watched her eyes fill with happy tears. "I am so happy for you, Kendi! I knew great things were in store for you this summer. We will have to talk more about this after lunch."

Emma and Hope were walking together, and Emma was chatting enthusiastically about their invitation to the water park party. "Can you get off work that day?" Emma asked Hope.

"Yeah! I don't usually work Sundays because Uncle Joe has a couple employees who cover weekends so that they can get discounts on renting boats for fishing."

"Oh, that's great," Emma said, "I'll text Mr. Femley to see if I can have that day off before he gets that week's schedule posted. I do NOT want to miss that party!"

"Amie, how about you?" Emma questioned. "Are you going to be able to go to the party at the water park?"

"I'll probably be able to hit part of it," Amie responded. "Sunday is a busy day with checkouts, so it tends to be all hands on deck. In fact, I'm heading there now. I'll ask if my aunt thinks I can escape early that Sunday."

◊ ◊◊◊ ◊

After lunch, Amie headed off to work, and the three other girls and Nola sat in the living room together.

"How did the concerts go? I haven't heard much about them yet," Aunty Nola asked.

"They were so great," Hope said, more animated than they had seen her before. "EVERYONE was there...well, everyone our age," she corrected.

"The music was great, the coffee was great, lots of people–it was super fun!" Emma agreed.

"And Kendi sang duets both nights," Hope went on. "You and Ben were awesome singing 'A Whole New World.' It was just like the movie," she smiled at Kendi.

"I really liked the duet from Grease that you and Ryan sang. You seemed like a real couple," Emma said, hoping deep down that Kendi would choose Ryan as the object of her affections, leaving Ben available.

"Thanks for your compliments, but I'm not in a couple with anyone. But I was excited to have the chance to sing in the coffee shop. That was my summer dream, and it happened week one," Kendi said humbly.

"Well, that's lovely," Aunty Nola beamed. "And what did you ladies think about church today?" she asked. "I know it was meaningful to Kendi, but what about you, Hope?"

"I'm really happy for Kendi, but I still have questions," Hope admitted. "I want to learn more about it this summer during our morning talks."

"We will definitely have more of those talks, Hope. We can pull out the Bible, and we can learn together," Aunty Nola assured her. "How about you, Emma? What did you think of church today?"

"It's so different from what I've heard before about religion. I definitely want to keep going to church and hear more." Emma stated.

Kendi just sat quietly while they talked.

Pretty soon after their conversation, Hope and Emma decided to take a walk by the lake. Kendi was still tired from working her late nights, so she stayed home to rest. She talked a little bit with Nola about the Bible, and then she went up to her room and laid down on her bed, feeling the sunshine and the breeze that flowed through her window that lulled her into a blissful nap.

CHAPTER ELEVEN
Waterpark Fun

Two weeks passed quickly for the girls as they worked lots of hours at their jobs and spent social time at the beach park.

Kendi and Ben didn't see each other too much because Kendi worked opening shifts and Ben worked later in the day. Kendi was still curious about the weird trip home on Saturday night of Memorial Day weekend, but she didn't spend too much time thinking about it. She'd been spending time reading her Bible that Aunty Nola had given her and lying in the sun with whichever of her friends were free on any given afternoon. She also spent time trying to text with her best friend Bella and talking to her parents. Connecting with Bella was an uphill battle. She rarely responded to Kendi's texts, and when she did, she always had an excuse about having to leave after just a few messages were exchanged. Kendi figured that things were a little off now since she was in Chelan, but hopefully, everything would be back to normal in the fall.

Kendi told her parents about her decision to follow Christ, and they were happy for her. "I want to be baptized at the lake when our church does baptisms at the Fourth of July service," Kendi said softly over the phone.

"That will be wonderful! We'll be there to celebrate with you, honey," her mom said with joy in her voice. "We really missed the mark with our own church attendance, and you have inspired us. Your dad and I want to look for a church to attend when you are back in town." Kendi was happy to hear that.

In texts, Bella had said that she had met an older boy named Mike when she was hanging out with a girl named Tonya. Kendi knew Tonya a little bit from school, and she knew that Tonya was a major partier. Kendi wasn't thrilled that Bella was hanging out with that particular group, and she wished that Bella could find nice friends like the ones Kendi had made at The Guesthouse.

"Did you still want to come on the Fourth of July weekend?" Kendi asked through finger strokes across the keyboard. "You can stay in my room. Amie will be staying in her cousin's room near the resort when he's at boy scout camp, and Hope's mom will be staying in Amie's room. My parents and Emma's parents have booked other rooms, so it's all settled. I can't wait for you to meet everyone!"

"Any cute boys?" Bella texted back.

"Plenty of really nice boys," Kendi assured her. "You'll see. GTG. C ya L8r," It made Kendi cringe, but she knew Bella liked to use text shorthand, so she used it on occasion.

"B4N," Bella texted back.

◊ ◊◊◊ ◊

The water park party day had finally arrived. The girls hurried home after church to get ready.

"I thought you had to work today?" Hope commented after noticing Amie in their midst.

"I got lucky. I'm so glad. I did NOT want to miss this party," Amie gushed excitedly.

"What are you going to wear?" Hope asked Amie.

"I think I'll wear my blue and white striped tankini with my white lace coverup over it, but I'll bring a change of clothes with my navy Calvin Klein shorts, this white V-neck top, and my Hollister sweatshirt in case it gets cold during the bonfire."

"That's a good idea." Hope laughed at herself inwardly for even asking the question because she realized that whatever Amie would have answered would not have changed what she was going to wear.

When it came to wardrobes, Amie and Hope could not be more different. Hope had very few clothes; most of them had come from the sports camps she had attended. Amie had matching accessories for every single outfit, including brand-name bags, bracelets, hair ties, and everything in between. To be fair, she had earned a lot of the money for her wardrobe by babysitting neighborhood kids and her cousin when her aunt and uncle worked long hours at the resort.

Hope slipped a pair of blue shorts on over her swim suit, put on a white t-shirt she had gotten at one of her sports camps, and grabbed a zipping sweatshirt that was part of her volleyball warm ups. Amie offered to stash Hope's beach towel and sweatshirt with her extra clothes in her tropical-looking Tommy Bahama bag, and Hope agreed, handing the clothes over.

Amie's family might have a lot of money, but Amie definitely was down to earth, very kind, and generous, Hope decided.

Kendi and Emma emerged from their rooms and sat down at the table where Aunty Nola had sub sandwiches for them. "I hope you like these sandwiches. When you were getting ready, I got them from the sandwich shop. I got the club sandwiches for Emma and Amie, turkey and cheddar for Hope and me, and salami for Kendi. I hope I remembered everybody's favorite."

The girls assured Aunty Nola that their sandwiches were perfect.

"Did you all remember to bring sunscreen? And a sweatshirt or jacket for later?" Aunty Nola bustled about, making sure her girls had everything they needed.

"Yes, Aunty Nola," they chorused, nearly in perfect unison.

"I'm ready to take you whenever you all are ready to go!" Aunty Nola said energetically.

The girls piled into the white van, and they drove to the entrance to town where the water park was located.

"Just text me when you are ready to come home," said Aunty Nola. "I'll be at a game night with some friends until about 9:00 this evening, but if you need me come before that, I can blow them off no problem."

The girls laughed at the youthful way Aunty Nola spoke for someone who was 70 years old. She never failed to surprise them.

The girls got to the park, and Kendi passed out the special orange wrist bands that Ben had given her at work the previous day. This allowed the girls to enter the park at no charge and to stay after hours for the special event. Ben had explained that Ryan's family did this once every summer for the high school students from church and their friends. They would be able to use all the attractions all afternoon. Then, when the park closed, they could continue for another hour or so with no lines, have dinner, and then Ryan's dad would give a short message.

The girls helped each other attach their wrist bands, and then they went up to the admission gate to borrow scissors to snip off the extra vinyl.

As the four girls entered the park, Hope noticed how vivid the freshly mowed grass looked and how it contrasted with the bright blue sky. She heard the squeals of children going down the slides and smelled the fragrance of hot dogs cooking on the grill and the sugary cotton candy in the concessions area.

Amie led them to the lockers, and they fit the two bags in one locker, so they only needed to have one key that Kendi clipped to the strap of her swimsuit.

From there, the girls threw their towels down on four lounge chairs that they were lucky enough to snatch as a family of four was packing up and leaving.

"Which slide should we do first?" Hope asked Amie.

"Definitely this one," Amie declared, grabbing a inflated bright yellow inner tube and heading up a steep paved path, her white-blonde bob bouncing as she walked. Each of the girls grabbed tubes and climbed up towards the top behind dozens of other eager sliders.

About a half hour later, they finally got all the way to the front of the line, and they had a choice between three slides, each with varying degrees of intensity. Amie and Hope chose the extreme intensity slide that had a startling steep decline, and Kendi and Emma chose the lane that promised medium intensity and included several exciting twists and turns. They each emerged in the pool at the bottom and couldn't wait to climb the hill and stand in line for another turn.

After they rode all those slides, they tried out the other set. These slides did not use inner tubes, so the girls were glad to not have to haul big tubes up the hill. The lines for these slides were also really long, but the thrill of the ride was worth it.

After their third go-around, the girls decided to make their way to the lazy river. At the entrance to the river, they saw some lime-green tandem tubes that were shaped like a figure 8 with a spot for two riders to sit. Amie and Hope commandeered one tube and Kendi and Emma situated themselves in another tube and they all relaxed as they floated around the man-made pool/river which snaked through the park.

As they floated, they could see people who were seated in different areas of the water park. A lot of people knew Amie and called out to her as she floated by.

"Wow, you are so popular," Emma said wistfully.

"Everybody's popular when you grow up in a small town," Amie said with a laugh. "We've all known each other since we were toddlers."

"I never thought I'd want to live in a small town," Emma confessed, "but I really love it here in Chelan."

"Spend a winter here, and you might feel differently," Amie remarked. "It's a cold and snowy ghost town except for skiers passing through. Some skiers stay in Chelan, but they leave before the sun comes up and return in the dark, so the town still looks empty during the day. Sometimes, when tourists come, the whole family doesn't go skiing, so we still have a few extra people around who eat at our lunch counter and go to the other restaurants and stores in town. But Chelan is a totally different place when it isn't summer."

"I'm not sure I'd like the winters as much as the summers," Emma began, "but I'd like to try!"

"Maybe someday you can," Hope stated. "My uncle started out as summer help, and he ended up coming back full-time and owning his own business."

"That's so cool! I'd love to interview your uncle for my business blog," Emma said excitedly.

"I'm sure he wouldn't mind. I'll talk to him about it." Hope told her.

"Looks like we're just about to get to our exit," Kendi stated. "Should we lay in the sun awhile?"

The girls agreed and they stretched out on their beach towels over the loungers they'd claimed earlier and relaxed.

Their relaxation was soon interrupted by a male voice that sounded like a radio announcer: "The Guesthouse Girls are in the hou-sssse!"

The girls looked up to see Ryan standing near them displaying his signature smile. They laughed and said hello.

"Thank you for our wristbands," Kendi said. "This park is great!"

"You're welcome! What would a party be without a bunch of beautiful young ladies?" Ryan asked. "You're staying after, aren't you?"

"Of course!" Amie replied. "I've been excited for this since last summer!" Then, turning to the other girls, she said, "NO LINES–is the best!"

"Well, you girls just relax and enjoy the sun, and you can ride the slides once the park is closed. Does anyone want a slushy on the house?" he asked all the girls while keeping his eyes on Kendi.

"Yes, please!" the girls replied with enthusiasm.

Ryan took their drink orders and soon returned with some napkins and straws and two black cherry slushies for Emma and Amie, a lime one for Hope, and a root beer slushy for Kendi. The girls thanked him, and he flashed them a dazzling smile and went back to work preparing for the afterparty.

"Ryan's a really nice guy," Amie remarked. "He really seems to like you, Kendi. Are you interested in him?"

"I don't know. I'm more focused on God right now," Kendi admitted. "I think I want to get more solid in that area before I get involved with a boy." Kendi said as Amie nodded approvingly.

"I wish I could have that kind of attitude," Emma said with a pout. "All the boys like Kendi, and she doesn't even care. I wish I had that kind of confidence."

"Well, Emma, you were turning plenty of boys' heads today." Amie commented. "Your skin is already a gorgeous color, and your curls are always perfectly bouncy, wet or dry."

"Thank you, Amie. I guess I am lucky to have naturally dark skin, and I'm very fortunate that my hair never seems to frizz up. Maybe I should focus on the positive instead of the negative?"

"I think we all tend to want what we can't have," Amie assured her. "I used to cry all the time because I was so short. I was always placed on the end of thefront row for the class picture when they arranged kids shortest to tallest. I felt like I was a loser or a baby. There was never any question about it, and I hated it. I always had a frowny face in the pictures because I was so miffed," she said laughing at the memory.

"I've always been tall, but I wanted longer arms and legs," Hope revealed, "Great athletes have long limbs."

"Well, having average legs and arms for your height hasn't seemed to stop you," Emma commented. "It seems like you're an amazing athlete regardless."

"Thanks, Emma," Hope laughed. "No matter what we have, we long for more."

"My problem is being average," Kendi joined in. "I'm not tall *or* short, I'm not model thin like Hope, and I don't have perfect curves like Emma. I don't even have that beautiful platinum blonde hair like Amie. I'm just … average. But," she said with a pause, "I'm beginning to think that's perfectly fine."

"You'd better believe it's fine!" cried Emma. "You have boys fighting to be with you!"

"Well, hopefully not literally," Kendi said with a laugh.

Hope asked the girls if anyone wanted to take another run at an inner tube slide. Kendi agreed, but Amie and Emma decided to sit this run out. Hope and Kendi went to grab tubes and get in line.

Amie took this opportunity to continue the conversation with Emma. "Emma, do you know how much God loves you?" she asked.

"If He really knows everything, He probably doesn't even like me," Emma contended.

"I guarantee He loves you, Emma. You are God's special princess. He made you in His image. Before you were even born, He made you exactly the way you're meant to be, and you are precious in His sight. However, it's up to us if we allow Him to clean up our sinful hearts so we can be just as beautiful on the inside.

He is willing to wash all our sins and ugliness away and make us new. We just need to ask Him."

"No offense, but your insides probably don't need any cleaning out. You are so friendly and kind to everyone, and you don't have a bad bone in your body."

"Emma, if only you knew how bad I am without Christ. When we're Christians, we still sin. The Bible says that His mercies are new every morning, so we need to confess our sins to Him regularly so He can continue to forgive us and change us so we can look more like Him. When we Christians don't do that, we can deteriorate and act just like the world around us. That's why people get disillusioned by the church and sometimes think that Christians are not any different than everyone else."

"Yeah, but what about you, Amie? I still have a hard time believing that you sin at all."

"Okay, just so you know that I'm telling the truth, let me tell you about sins that I commit on the regular and need to confess. Just when I think I'm growing in one area, another sin pattern starts to pop up. Sins are like fast-growing weeds, and they have to be plucked regularly.

"One of the areas that I need to grow in is honoring my parents. It's one of the Ten Commandments, and between you and me, I'm terrible at that one. I always question what they say; sometimes, I roll my eyes at them and say things under my breath. In fact, that's why I don't get to drive this summer, even though I have my driver's license. I mouthed off once too often to my parents, and that was my punishment and unfortunately, I deserved it."

"Okay, so you're a normal kid. We're all like that with our parents. What else do you do that makes you not perfect?" Emma pressed.

"Well, I tend to be a judgmental person about a lot of things. For example, school comes really easy to me, so I get frustrated and judgmental of people who struggle. When some students ask questions and delay progress in the class, I get frustrated. Sometimes, I try to catch the eye of other people who I know feel the same way, and we roll our eyes and quietly laugh at the person who's trying to learn by asking questions." Amie sighed. "I know that's extremely out of line. The only reason I am good at school is because God blessed me with a brain that is good at most school subjects.

"I'm terrible at learning things outside of school, like driving a car. Here's a secret: I took driver's ed, but I did so poorly that I had to pay extra to get extended driving lessons before they would let me pass the course, and even then, my dad had to talk to the driver's ed teacher to assure him that I would get lots of help from him before I sat for the driver's test. If kids in my class knew about that, they would roll their eyes and laugh and make fun of me, just like I did to kids in math class.

"Emma, that's just a taste of some of the sins I commit that I need forgiveness for, and I've been a Christian for ten years. But God is kind and forgiving, and He cleans us and heals us on the inside. The Bible tells us that He removes our sins from us as far as the East is from the West…we just need to ask. When I sin like the ways I've told you, I need to confess what I did to Jesus, tell Him I'm sorry, and then try to change and not do it again, or at least do it less often. If you hear the pastor talk about 'repentance,' that's what that is."

"Wow, you seem so perfect. It's actually such a relief to know that you have flaws, too. Thanks for telling me all that, Amie. I appreciate how open you were about this."

"No problem, Emma. I might look put-together on the outside, but just below the surface is ugliness that needs to be cleansed daily, if not even more often." Amie said. She then consulted the large digital clock on the arch above the park entrance. They should be closing the park to the public any time now I can't wait to go on the slides without the lines."

Just then, the loudspeaker announced that the park would be closing in ten minutes, and everyone should gather up their things and proceed to the exit.

"Except uuuuuussssss," Amie said in a singsong voice, and Emma laughed in agreement.

The girls left their chairs and wandered around the park, which was quickly emptying. Emma noticed that almost all the kids she had met this summer were present. Amie and Emma walked up to Hannah and Evan, who Emma met in the park the second night they were there, and they began a conversation about Pasco, Emma's hometown.

Amie found a few people she knew from the resort–Josh, Tanner, and Angie–and started talking to them.

"Hey, Josh! You must've had an early shift," she said.

"Yeah, I missed church today because I worked breakfast in the dining room and lunch at the lunch counter. I finished up the orders and jetted over here."

"Well, it seems like you're always working, so I'm not surprised that they were willing to let you leave. I'm sure they appreciate all the hours you put in," Angie, a girl who worked in the kitchen, commented.

"I appreciate them, too," Josh said, looking at Amie with an awkward smile.

"How about you, Tanner?" Amie asked.

"Uh, I appreciate your family, too..." he said tentatively.

"No, I mean did you work at the Beaches today?"

"Oh yeah, I did. I caught a ride here with Josh."

"You guys want to ride the Intensity Slide?" Amie changed the subject, grinning.

"Lead the way," Josh said as he and his friends followed Amie to grab tubes and make the trek to the steep ride that Amie and Hope enjoyed earlier.

As they were walking, they heard some loud Christian music fill the park. The music started out with the familiar intro from the song "Jesus Freak," recorded by DC Talk before the teens were even born. The music and lyrics always had wide appeal and got the party started. Song after song followed, transforming the water park into almost a concert atmosphere. All the kids were whizzing down slides without having to wait in line, and there were just a few kids slowly floating around the park in the winding lazy river.

Emma had a lot to think about, she felt a little cold, so she found a large Jacuzzi to hang out in. The beat of the music was good for her, and she found herself moved by the lyrics. She really got lost in her thoughts; Amie had opened up her mind to the possibility that God might actually love her, even though she felt that she was so ugly and snarky on the inside. She always thought that Christians were the "perfect" people, like Aunty Nola, Ben, and Amie.

However, tonight, Amie helped her see that Christians weren't perfect…just forgiven. She was all alone with her thoughts in the warm, bubbly water.

Pretty soon, Ben entered the large hot tub. He waved at her, and she made her way over to him.

"How are you, cutie?" he asked her while flashing his irresistible smile.

She blushed under Ben's compliment. "I'm having fun!" she replied. "This was so nice of Ryan's family."

"I know, right?" he agreed. "I'm looking forward to eating. They'll have a full barbecue grill set up in a little while with hot dogs and hamburgers," Ben said, gesturing towards the patio area across the park.

"That sounds good," Emma murmured. Normally, she would have killed for alone time with Ben in the jacuzzi. However, tonight was different; she needed to be away from boys to get some things figured out. She surprised herself by stepping up the stairs, right past Ben and exiting the hot tub, calling to him from over her shoulder, "I'm going to see if Ryan's mom needs help setting food out. Nice to see you, Ben, see ya later!"

Ben shrugged at her quick exit, watched her as she walked away, and then stretched out in the hot tub to relax.

Emma reached the patio area and introduced herself to Ryan's mom, Tiffany. She was soon busy helping her carrying buns to the men who were grilling the burgers and dogs.

She had a nice conversation with Tiffany when they were assembling the condiment trays. They discussed the history of the water park, and Emma asked her if she and her husband would be willing to be interviewed for her business blog. Tiffany thought it would be fun and asked Emma if she was staying at The Guesthouse. Emma acknowledged that she was.

"Oh, my son was talking about a girl who lives there. Was that you?"

"No, I think he was probably talking about my roommate Kendi. I think they've talked to each other a few times."

"Well, I know that Nola always selects really nice girls to stay at The Guesthouse. She has a knack for knowing who will fit in well."

"I think you're right. Me and the other girls are already like sisters. We're all different, but we get along well and it seems like we've known each other forever!"

"That's great! Hey, let's go grab the trays of those amazing cupcakes out of the cooler, and we can put them at the end of the buffet table, if you don't mind?"

With that, they went off to grab the delicious, chocolatey creations that had been delivered by Rachel from Brandon's Coffee and Bakeshop earlier that day.

Pretty soon, the loudspeaker came on and Ryan's dad announced to the 80 teens in the park that the slides would be closing soon, everyone should dry off and get dressed, and then make their way to the buffet tables and grab some dinner.

Kendi, Hope, and Amie finished up the slide they were on and went to their locker to grab their bags. They saw Ben at the lockers and asked if he had seen Emma, and he pointed them in the direction of the food tables. Hope jogged over and got Emma so they could change.

"Brrr, are you freezing?" Hope asked.

"Now that you mention it, I am," Emma said. "I'll be glad to cover up a bit." Soon, all the girls were dressed and ready for dinner.

They went through the buffet line and grabbed their food and some drinks and sat down. Ben and Ryan sat down with them, and soon, Cody came by as well. Conner and Brett joined their circle, as did Hannah, Evan, and Drew. Josh and his friends sat nearby, as well as many other kids that Amie knew from church and school. There was a lot of laughter and fun as they ate their dinner.

"There's nothing like a day in the sun to make you hungry," Ben said, holding his stomach.

"You were born hungry," someone called out, and the group laughed.

"Nothing a couple of mom's cupcakes can't fix," Ben retorted with a smile, licking some of the heap of frosting off his cupcake.

Ryan's dad's voice came over the loudspeaker encouraging everyone to find a seat around the fire pit. Ryan led the group over to the far corner of the property where the fire pit was uncovered and ignited.

The sun was fully down at this point, and the girls pulled on their sweatshirts to combat the cooler temperature. Emma sat down between Hope and Kendi. Amie sat on the other side of Kendi.

How lucky I am to have this group of friends, Emma thought.

Ben's brother Joseph and one of his friends brought out guitars and led the group in some worship songs. They played a song that Emma had heard at church last week called "Reckless Love." It had touched her heart when she'd first heard it. As Emma read the words on the screen at church, she was so moved by the words that God's love pursues people. There was a reference to 99 that Emma didn't understand and she made a mental note to ask Amie or Auntie Nola about what that meant.

The next song had descriptive phrases about who God was and the amazing roles that He played in people's lives. He could work miracles, and give light where we needed it. The chorus repeated the phrases often enough that Emma was able to memorize this song, and that made her happy since many of the songs the other kids sang, she had never heard before.

Emma saw that some of the kids, including Amie, were closing their eyes when they sang the lyrics, and some were even raising their hands in worship. She was impressed that they felt strongly enough about their faith that they weren't embarrassed to worship, even in front of their peers.

Amie requested the next song called "Living Hope." Ryan's dad commented that was very appropriate for what he was going to talk about. They sang this song, and Emma hung on to every word. She loved it when the kids triumphantly sang the title phrase, addressing it to Jesus. She found herself singing loudly with the group

When Ryan's dad started giving his message, he explained things that answered some of the questions that Emma had wondered about.

He talked about how sheep are not very smart animals. He then said that people are sometimes compared to sheep in the Bible, and Jesus is the Great Shepherd. He said if a shepherd had 100 sheep, and one of them wandered away, the shepherd would leave the 99 sheep behind, go get the one sheep, and bring him back to the flock where he would be safe, because the sheep wouldn't have a chance out there on their own.

"Have you ever thought that you are that lost sheep?" Ryan's dad asked the crowd. "You are out there on your own trying to figure out life, and you may have gotten yourself in some trouble along the way. The truth is that we all have been that lost sheep, but Jesus is the great Shepherd. He wants to find you and bring you into the flock where you can be safe. The boundaries He sets for Christians are not to keep us from having fun and freedom but to allow us to have protection from the evils around us. God isn't just interested in having the popular people, or the beautiful people, or the people who are really good. The Bible says that God is not willing that *any* should perish, but all come to repentance. He says that if we confess our sins, He is faithful and just and will forgive our sins and cleanse us from all unrighteousness. Maybe this is your night. Maybe you are the sheep He is searching for. If that is the case, I challenge you to be courageous and stand during the next song. This could be your first time acknowledging your need for a Savior, or it could be your millionth…God is still there for you."

Emma's heart was thumping because she knew that this was her night, and she needed to stand up, but she was scared and wondered what people would think of her. She wondered what would come next for her if she took this step. The speaker had warned that she would never be the same.

The guitars started playing a song that Emma guessed was called "How Great is Our God," and the group began to sing. The chorus of this song was really easy for Emma to pick up. By the time it had been sung through the first time, Emma was shaking. Even though she trembled, she found herself standing. To her surprise, she saw others rising as well while they sang the beautiful anthem. By the end of the song, half the group was on their feet.

After the song finished, Ryan's mom Tiffany took all of the girls who were standing to another area, and Ryan's dad took all the boys who stood to a different part of the park. Ben's brother Joseph sat with the others and played more songs and the kids who remained seated sang.

Emma and the other girls sat on lounge chairs together, and Tiffany seated herself in front of them. She told them that she wanted to lead them in prayer and asked if anyone wanted to ask Jesus into her life for the first time.

Emma raised her hand and a couple other hands came up, too.

Tiffany led the group in a prayer, first with the girls who were asking Jesus for salvation, and then with the girls who were needing to rededicate themselves to pursuing God. Tiffany had told the girls that if they had prayed that prayer, they had just become part of a bigger family, the family of God. When she was finished, Emma opened her eyes and went back to join her friends at the fire.

She received hugs from Amie, Kendi, and even Hope. Emma felt very happy that she had made her choice. Now, all she could think about was telling her parents and her little sister Rylie about it. She hoped Rylie would also want to become a Christian.

◊ ◊◊◊ ◊

Later, Aunty Nola came to pick them up. On the way home, Amie announced, "Emma has some big news!"

"Is it about a boy?" Aunty Nola teased.

"Much more important than that," Kendi gushed.

"I asked Jesus into my life." Emma said softly.

"Oh, Emma, I want to hear all about it."

When they got home, they sat around the table while Emma shared with them how she came to her decision. Aunty Nola promised to get her a Bible and asked Emma if she would like to get baptized so she could demonstrate publicly that she was a Christian.

"I think that would be great, especially since my parents will be here and I can do it with Kendi."

"And we'll all be there to support you!" Amie smiled.

"Well, it's all settled, then," Aunty Nola concluded. "Make sure tell your parents. They'll want to know."

"Okay," Emma agreed.

The girls then told Aunty Nola all about their day at the water slides before all four girls went up to bed.

CHAPTER TWELVE
A Disastrous Day at the Bakeshop

Kendi's alarm woke her up at 5 a.m. She pushed snooze and decided to skip her morning shower. Moments later, she thought better of it, turned off her snooze, and dragged herself to the shower.

Feeling refreshed, she put on some mascara and some lip gloss and dressed in a black skort and a dark green polo shirt with the logo for Brandon's Coffee & Bakeshop in the top left. She put on some cute, slip-on shoes with a heel and headed to work. She told herself she didn't wear these shoes to just look cute for Ben. However, she wasn't sure if she even convinced herself.

This was going to be a special shift because Mr. Brandon, who allowed the young staff to call him Mark, was doing an experimental day to see which specialty drink they were going to offer this week. He had invited Kendi to come in early and create three new drinks, and they would taste them and decide which ones to offer. Kendi's creative juices were flowing, and she was ready to put forth some contenders.

When she arrived at the shop, Mark and one other employee, Bonnie, were already there. "Change of plans," he announced grimly. "Rachel's dad had a stroke, and Rachel and Ben are on their way to Wenatchee to be with him and her mom. We are going to have you work in the bake shop today. Rachel thought you could do a few of the recipes, so we will have something to serve our customers. I'll help you figure out which ones to do. Do you feel comfortable doing that, Kendi?"

"Sure," she said, not at all confident in her baking, but more eager to help in Rachel's place. "I'm so sorry about Rachel's dad! Is he going to be okay?"

"It's too soon to tell," Mark reported. "Reed is going to come in later today to work, and Joseph and I will head to Wenatchee to be with the family."

"I can stay late if you need me to. Just tell me what would be helpful."

"Thanks, Kendi. Let's play that part by ear. It looks like we have several croissants, tarts, and enough savories in the case, so we can probably get by with baking a large batch of giant muffins and maybe some cowboy cookies. If you have time, maybe you could also do a batch of brownies, too? We are a little behind, and we need to get something out for the morning rush."

"No problem," Kendi replied, heading to the hand-washing sink. She longed to text Ben and see how he was doing, and get an update on his grandpa, but that would have to wait.

She pulled out the recipe binder and removed the plastic sleeve that enclosed the lemon poppy seed recipe. She busied herself adding the wet ingredients in the large professional floor stand metal mixing bowl and turned it on so the ingredients could blend. She went back to the counter and carefully measured the flour, baking soda, and other dry ingredients into a large bowl according to the recipe directions. She was feeling proud of the way she was taking care of things all by herself...

...But suddenly, she realized she had forgotten to add the flavoring. She ran back to the shelf where the flavorings were kept and hustled back across the kitchen, opening the bottle to add the lemon flavor to the other wet ingredients.

Unfortunately, in her haste to stay on schedule, she slipped in her fancy shoes, and her elbow caught the bowl of dry ingredients, sending it flying across the kitchen. In a moment that felt like it moved in slow motion, the metal bowl rocketed into the air. Kendi watched in horror as it spun end over end mid-air, and she was powerless to do anything about it. The bowl crashed to the ground with a thud, but not before bouncing on the countertop and dislodging the contents of the bowl. The flour mixture went everywhere, covering the rack of baking pans, the cookbook shelf, the metal counter, and the floor.

Kendi needed to get this cleaned up before anyone came back and saw her incompetence. She looked frantically for the broom.

Just then, the buzzer went off indicating that the oven was preheated. Kendi decided that it was more important to get the muffins in the oven than to clean up the mess at the moment, so she took the now empty metal bowl and again carefully measured the flour for another round.

Once again, she remembered that she had forgotten to add the lemon flavoring. She went back to retrieve it from where it had landed after the flour incident. She realized that it was half empty at this point, but there was just enough for the batch she was making. She dumped it in to get it mixed into the batter. She oh-so-carefully grabbed the bowl with the flour and added it to the mixer. She measured out the poppy seeds and added them last.

"Whew," she sighed to herself as she spooned the last of the batter into the muffin tins and slid them in the oven. "I'll get started with the brownies, try to clean up quickly, and–hopefully–no one will see the mess I made."

She turned around to get started with the brownies, then she noticed the baking soda container sitting on the counter.

"Uh oh. I think I forgot to add that to the second bowl of flour," she moaned. "Or did I?"

Kendi second-guessed herself a few times, then determined that she had definitely forgotten to add the baking soda. She tried to figure out how to recover from this huge oversight. She hastily pulled the hot muffin tins out of the oven. They had barely started to cook, and the top was just starting to glaze over. She hoped she had retrieved them in time.

She started her recovery mission by spooning the warm batter from the muffin tin into a bowl. She was about halfway through, and it was taking a lot of time. She thought, *Maybe I can use half the baking soda and add it to this half of the batter. Then, I can just add the other half to the muffins that are already in the tins to save time.* So, she proceeded to follow this plan, adding baking soda to the batter that she had scraped out of the tins. She then put that tin back in the oven. Lastly, she took a tiny bit of baking soda and stirred it into each of the remaining muffins individually.

Maybe some of the muffins will be salvageable, she thought as she turned on the timer for five minutes less than the original time on the recipe sheet.

Kendi cleaned out the big metal mixing bowl and started in on the brownies. She was extremely cautious as she measured out each ingredient one by one. The brownie batter looked great to her, so she poured it into a sheet pan to be baked in oven number two. Kendi noticed that she had forgotten to preheat the oven, and it was still cold. She decided she'd better get them in the oven anyway, so she put them in and turned the oven on a little hotter than normal to speed things up.

Mr. Brandon called back, "How's it going back there?"

Kendi rushed to the flapping door that separated the kitchen from the cashier and espresso area. She poked her head out, hoping he wouldn't need to come back.

"It's going well! Muffins and brownies are both in the oven, and I'm just starting on the cookies now."

"Great job, Kendi. We've been slammed up here. The baked goods from yesterday are almost gone."

"Okay! I'll get it stocked as soon as I can," Kendi replied, glad to see a long line for coffee, which meant that neither Mark nor Bonnie would be able to come to the back anytime soon.

Nevertheless, just as she was adding chocolate chips to the big mixer, Kendi saw the flapping door move and saw Reed heading to the back to grab her apron.

"What the heck happened?" Reed asked incredulously. "Looks like you had an explosion."

"I kind of did," Kendi admitted. "But *shhh*, I want to get this cleaned up before anyone sees this. Mark doesn't need one more thing to add to everything else they have going on right now."

Reed nodded. "I think he's about to leave for Wenatchee. I'll try to keep him from coming back here."

"Thanks," Kendi mouthed gratefully as Reed headed back to the front.

Kendi scooped the cookie dough into perfect spheres and brought the trays to the walk-in freezer to chill. She noticed there was already chilled cookie dough back there, and she could have just baked the ones that were already in the freezer and not had to make new dough.

"Argg! Could this day get any worse?" Kendi sighed.

Then, she realized it could.

The timer went off, and she went to the oven to retrieve the muffins, not sure what she would find.

146

They were what she would call a hot mess.

The muffins that actually rose were lopsided, and the other ones were flat and didn't have a muffin top at all.

"What a disaster!" she whined, then quickly clammed up, hoping the rest of the staff didn't hear her.

She put the poor muffins on the counter to cool. She tasted one of the uglier ones because she didn't waste one that might be sellable. It tasted fine to her, so she decided she would try to salvage some of them.

She let them cool while she went to get the already chilled cookie dough that someone must have made yesterday. She waited for the oven to preheat, and then popped a tray in and set the timer. She also found the broom and swept up most of the flour mess.

Kendi heard the timer ring and pulled the brownie tray out of the oven. They didn't look as fluffy as normal, but they still looked like brownies. Kendi let them cool while she chose six of the best-looking muffins from the ragtag group and brought them up front to add to the case.

"Looks like she went to battle with the flour," one of the customers noted.

Bonnie looked at Kendi, "Apparently the flour won."

Reed shot Kendi a look of sympathy when she saw the lopsided muffins.

Kendi, unable to afford the time to make her case for the deflated muffins, returned to the back room and heard the timer ring for the cookies. They looked perfect. She took them out of the oven and put them on the rack to cool.

She used the cutting tool that fit over the tray of brownies and cut them into perfect rectangles. This time, the cutting process didn't go quite as smoothly as it did when she did it with Rachel. She applied a little more pressure, and the brownies were cut. She grabbed about six of them brought them to the display case.

Even though the items didn't look perfect, Kendi was glad to have actually produced something that they could sell. This gave her a glimmer of satisfaction.

She went to the back room to grab some cookies to put out. The giant cookies looked perfect. She grabbed twelve of them to fill the case so, hopefully, people would ignore the other items.

Satisfied, Kendi went to the backroom to finish cleaning up all the flour. She decided to taste the brownies and realized they were super hard on the bottom, the result of putting them into a cool oven instead of a preheated one.

Reed came back to grab another sleeve of lids. Kendi grabbed her and asked her to try a bite of brownie. "They're too hard on the bottom! What should I do?" she whispered frantically.

"I like them that way," Reed said with a quick shrug. "They're pretty good."

At this, Kendi was relieved.

She dumped the muffins without tops in the garbage, then finished cleaning the kitchen and took the garbage out to the dumpster. She came back, washed her hands, and surveyed her display case. Several items had sold. She replenished the display case with more goodies.

After she refilled the case, Bonnie let Kendi know that she was going home, so Kendi would need to work up in the front with Reed until her shift was finished. Kendi was surprised to find that she only had one hour left. What a relief! She found that her hands were shaking from the stress of so many mistakes.

She assumed the position in front of the register and took coffee orders from customers. When people asked for a brownie, she made sure to tell them that they were fresh out of the oven, but a little hard on the bottom. Most people were okay with that and bought them anyway.

By the end of Kendi's shift, there were two croissants, one tart, three muffins, eight brownies, and several cookies left. That would be plenty to get them through the rest of the day and into tomorrow morning.

When Lynn came to do a closing shift at 3 o' clock, Kendi was more than happy to go home and couldn't get out of there fast enough.

She hurried home, closed her bedroom door, poured her heart out to God, and let the tears flow out of her eyes.

She heard a soft knock on her door and she murmured, "Come in."

Aunty Nola's feet padded across the floor and she came over and sat on Kendi's bed. "What's wrong, honey?" she asked with concern.

Kendi shared the whole story of her day of bakeshop blunders. When she was finished, she had fresh tears in her eyes. "I'm such a horrible baker," she moaned.

"They'll never trust me with any responsibility again. I hope they don't fire me."

"Oh Kendi, they certainly won't fire you. They know everyone makes mistakes. It sounds like you were able to make lemonade from your lemons today and you probably learned some good baking lessons, too."

"Yeah, I learned that I can't be trusted to bake!" she retorted with a slight grin.

"Well, I'm sure that if you ever have do the baking at work again, things will go well and you won't drop the bowl of flour.

"Yes, I will not wear shoes with heels, either," Kendi added.

"And, you'll preheat the oven ahead of time," Nola contributed to the list.

"And, I'll focus more on whether I added the baking soda already or not!" Kendi concluded.

"Well, it looks like you won't have to live in fear another disastrous day in the bakeshop," Aunty Nola assured her.

"Yeah, I guess so," Kendi mumbled.

"Is it okay if I pray for you?" Aunty Nola requested.

"That would be fantastic," Kendi replied.

Aunty Nola uttered a beautiful prayer thanking God for bringing Kendi to The Guesthouse this summer and asking Him to bathe Kendi in peace and to let every detail of this day at the bake shop bring glory to Him. She asked God to be with the Brandon family and with Rachel's dad as he continued to recover from his stroke and start therapy.

After Aunty Nola finished her prayer and went back downstairs, Kendi sank into a healing sleep as the breezes blew through her open window and the birds sang.

◊ ◊◊◊ ◊

Following her nap, Kendi woke up with a new perspective. At dinner that night, Kendi shared all the details of her day with her roommates. It was humbling for her, to say the least. The girls all reacted sympathetically.

"Oh Kendi, that must have been awful." Amie commiserated.

"Yeah," Hope agreed. "I'm sure you were worried about making your bosses think you can't handle things. But really, you completed what you set out to do. There were treats for customers to buy so you did your job," she stated.

Emma chimed in from a different point of view, "Kendi, your day was kinda like my day is every day. I screw up on everything I do, not intentionally, but that is kinda just who I am. I think it is easier for me to forgive myself because I make so many mistakes on the daily. If I beat myself up for all of them, I wouldn't get out of bed in the morning. I have always been jealous of girls like you who never seem to mess things up. But now I see that when people like you have a hard day, it is harder to shake it off because you don't have much experience with blunders."

"Well Emma, that *is* an interesting perspective,"

151

Aunty Nola smiled. "It is lovely to see how God gives us our own personalities, strengths, and weaknesses and He teaches us new lessons through all of them, if we take the time to learn."

The girls nodded in agreement.

"Now tell us again how that bowl of flour looked as it tumbled through the air," Amie teased and Kendi replied by tossing a wadded up linen napkin in her direction. The four roommates and Aunty Nola laughed until they cried thinking about poor Kendi's baking misadventures.

CHAPTER THIRTEEN
Emma's Blog Interview

Emma had a good day at work because she got to be
back at the ice cream counter. She enjoyed helping the
people select their flavors while scooping out perfect-
looking cones as she chatted with vacationers.

After her shift, she was going to go to Mr. Femley's
house tonight for dinner. His daughter Kim, who
worked at the store part-time, would be there with her
two young children. Mr. Femley had agreed to let
Emma interview him for her business blog after dinner.
He still wasn't sure what a business blog was, but he
was willing to share his story.

◊ ◊◊◊ ◊

That night at dinner, Emma got to know Kim a little
better. She mostly worked weekends, while Emma
rarely worked those days, so they didn't cross paths
much at the store. Emma was delighted with Titus and
Taylor, Kim's sons. They were only three and five years
old, but they were quite charming and well-behaved.

Their dad was in the army and was deployed overseas, so Kim and her kids had moved in with her dad for the summer.

Emma had an animated conversation with five-year-old Taylor, who explained his perspective on daddies and mommies who were in the military.

"You see, mommies and daddies who are soldiers are very tough, and they protect us. Sometimes, they are called heroes, because that's what they are," Taylor explained. My daddy is a hero cuz he defends our country so we can have fireworks," he concluded.

"Wow, Taylor! That's *so* cool. I actually have an older brother who's a soldier, too," Emma said proudly.

"Is he with my daddy?" little Titus asked in his high-pitched baby talk.

"No, Titus. I don't think they're together. I think he's at his base in Florida," Emma explained.

"Do you know how strong I am?" Taylor asked.

"No? How strong?" Emma asked, her eyes wide.

"Army Strong!" he said with a growl, and little Titus giggled.

"Oh, yeah," Emma agreed. "My brother Joey is Army Strong, too!"

"Wow, Emma! Have you done a lot of babysitting? You are great with kids!" Kim said approvingly.

"Yes! Babysitting the neighborhood kids back home is how I make my spending money," she replied.

"Hmmm…maybe we'll have to hit you up at some point," Kim said thoughtfully. "Dad and I might want to do something without the boys sometime."

"That'd be great. Titus and Taylor are so cute. I'd love to play with them sometime! Maybe you can drop them off at The Guesthouse and they can have four babysitters plus Aunty Nola?" Emma laughed.

"I'll keep that in mind," Kim promised her. "Now, boys," she turned to address her sons, "let's go watch a VeggieTales movie in the playroom so Miss Emma can talk to Grandpa."

Kim got the boys situated and then sat on the couch in the living room next to her dad. Emma told Mr. Femley that she would take notes. She also asked to record their conversation in case she missed anything, and Mr. Femley agreed.

Emma began by asking Mr. Femley to tell her when the store first opened.

Mr. Femley cleared his throat and began telling his story: "Back in the old days, Chelan was an even smaller town than it is now. It was really no more than a collection of farms built around the lake with a couple churches, bars, and a post office. People came to the store to trade their fruits, vegetables, and chickens for fabric and other dry goods. Eventually, the trading post turned into an actual store, and most of the farms gave way to tourism. The main street was paved, and the owner of the little store didn't seem to like paying taxes, so they eventually decided to sell the store to my grandpa. That is how my grandpa became the very first Mr. Femley to own the store, and he was really proud of it and renamed it Femley's Mercantile when he took possession of it, about 80 years ago."

Mr. Femley took a breath and continued: "My dad was a teenager when my grandpa bought the store, and he was expected to work all the time he was not in school. I believe he missed out on a lot of fun because he was always working...but I guess it paid off for him, because the store grew. By the time my grandpa passed away and my dad took over, the store had grown to include a soda fountain, a pharmacy, and a photo processing facility. It was actually a lot bigger back when I was a teenager. And yes, I had to work at the store, too, but not as much as my dad did. I actually got to play football at Chelan High and do other things kids did back then," he chuckled while remembering.

"As the town grew," he said, "somebody came and built a stand-alone pharmacy so we closed ours down. We also removed the soda fountain seating where teenagers used to hang out and just kept the counter where we serve the ice cream to go now. As far as the photo processing, we let that go as well, as that is a service no longer needed."

"I went off to college, ended up getting drafted, and served in Vietnam." He sighed heavily. "I spent a one-year tour there, and I came back a broken man...not physically, but mentally and emotionally. Before the war, I wanted to move to New York and take on the world, but when I came home, I just wanted to hide."

Emma could hear the brokenness in his voice, and her heart ached for him. She wasn't sure if she should say anything, but, against her nature, she decided to remain quiet and wait.

"I went into the service as an optimistic boy ready to take on the world, and came home just shattered," he rephrased. "The stress of the war affected many families, not just us. Some of my high school classmates lost their lives," he added sadly. "At that point, all I wanted to do was to hang on to something solid, and for me, that was my family and my town. I hunkered down here and began working at the store with my folks."

Then, his tone grew lighter. "I married a girl I knew from high school, and eventually, we had Kimmie and her older brother Robert. My wife Patty and I took over the business when my dad and mama retired about 25 years ago. With my folks' blessing, Patty and I changed the name from 'Mercantile' to 'General Store' because we thought 'mercantile' sounded too lofty, and we were just a little country store. Then, both my parents were killed in a motorhome accident when they were leaving on their first retirement trip." Mr. Femley paused, obviously reliving horrible memories that he hadn't thought about for a while.

"My wife Patty ended up getting breast cancer and passing away ten years ago," said Mr. Femley. "She never got to meet Taylor and Titus, but she did get to meet Robert's kids, and she loved them to pieces," he brightened at the thought. "My son Robert was never a fan of the store that took up all his parents' and grandparents' time and ruined his summers, and he always insisted vehemently that he would not be the next 'Mr. Femley' to take over Femley's General Store.

He left town as soon as he graduated from high school and came home only at Christmas and Thanksgiving so Patty could love on her grandchildren. Now that she is gone, he only comes back rarely. That is his choice, of course; he is busy with his family. That leaves Kimmie to take over the store, and she is busy with her husband and her boys, so I don't know if they will want to move here permanently and take this on. So far, they have not seemed too eager to do that," Mr. Femley stated. He cleared his throat. "I'm sorry, Emma, but this turned out to be more my story than the store."

"Mr. Femley, that's okay! I'm so happy to have heard your story. There's been so much pain in your life, and I never would have guessed it. You always show up cheerful and energetic and ready to take on whatever life throws at you," Emma stated admiringly. "How do you do that?"

"Well Emma, I'd have to say it is my faith. God's mercies are new every morning, and, if you think about it, there is always something to be thankful for."

"That's a great attitude," Emma said with a smile.

Emma proceeded to ask Mr. Femley specific questions about the store, what product lines sell the best, what has surprised him over the years, what were some funny things that have happened at the store, and more. Mr. Femley had an answer for every question, and Emma had a lot of good material for her blog.

She noticed how dark it was. About that time, Kim walked back into the room after checking on the boys. "It sounds like you're wrapping up," she observed.

"Yes! Emma has enough to fill up a book now," Mr. Femley laughed.

"How about if I give you a ride home, Emma? We can chat a little more about babysitting?" Kim asked warmly.

Emma had not relished the idea of walking home alone, so she was grateful that Kim had offered the ride.

◊ ◊◊◊ ◊

When she arrived home, Emma sat down with Aunty Nola, told her about her interview with Mr. Femley, and asked her if she ever knew his wife, Patty.

"Oh, my yes," replied Aunty Nola. "Patty and George–that is, Mrs. and Mr. Femley–and I all attended Chelan High together," she recounted. "He was an amazing athlete, and kind of loud and arrogant. All the girls wanted to date him. He received a full tuition scholarship to attend UCLA for athletics."

"He didn't say a word about that," Kendi mentioned.

"Well, that makes sense. When he came back from the war, he was crushed. He was no longer overconfident, and he was in bad shape mentally," Aunty Nola frowned.

"Then what happened?" Emma asked.

"Well, Patty invited him to go to church with her. He accepted Jesus, his walls started to melt, and he grew into the man he is now. Patty was my close friend for years, and I am so happy they had each other for as long as they did, but she got taken so soon. She was only fifty-nine."

"He's seen a lot of tragedy," Emma remarked.

"George Femley is a living testimony about the power of God in a person's life."

"Yes, he is," Emma stated as she looked at the time. "I'd better get to bed!"

"Goodnight, little one," Aunty Nola murmured.

"Goodnight," Emma replied and headed to her room.

CHAPTER FOURTEEN
Front Desk Fiascos

Amie showed up for her shift at the front desk, unaware that this would be anything but a normal day.

She logged on to her system and took over for Brenda, who worked the night shift. Brenda had mentioned that they were going to have twenty checkouts and at least sixteen arrivals today, so the housekeeping staff would be hopping. She said "housekeeping staff," but Amie knew that included the front desk staff; Amie and Linda would also be busy.

The first family to check in arrived at 8 o' clock in the morning. Normal check-in time was 3:00 p.m., but the dad of the family pressured the front desk gals and, since they had room 122 ready, they allowed the family to check in early so they could rest after driving all night from Oregon. Amie made sure they knew that this was a special exception to the policy of 3 o' clock check-ins and figured she wouldn't hear back from them again until they checked out several days later.

Boy, was she wrong.

From the moment the family checked in, they became what she would call "Guestzillas." They started out by complaining about the room because they could see the lake if they looked out the window in one direction, but if they looked in the other direction, there was no lake.

"This was not the panoramic view that I was promised online!" the man shouted from his phone. "I need an upgrade!"

Amie politely explained that they were fully booked, and no other rooms were available. She stopped short of pulling up the ad for the suite they saw online and pointing out how the cost of that suite was triple what this family paid for their room.

Next, the family called to complain that there were a lot of people at the pool closest to their room. Amie consulted the security screens and said, "You're in luck, Pool Three only has a few people."

The same guests complained that they had to walk all the way down to Pool Three to not have a crowded swimming pool. Amie assured them that the walk would only take about two to three minutes. That seemed to appease them for the moment.

Then, lunchtime came, and they complained that Beaches, the resort's lunch counter restaurant, was too crowded, and they had to eat in the outdoor seating, which was really hot, even under the shade. The lunch counter staff did their best to accommodate this demanding family, but they were determined to be unhappy. They even complained about the lunch special because they didn't like seafood.

Later, they grumbled to the front desk that all the paddleboards had been rented from the equipment shack. Amie calmly explained that the paddleboards are reserved days in advance, but they could make a reservation now and probably get one in the next couple days. This, of course, was not a satisfactory answer.

Amie remarked to Linda that they weren't even scheduled to officially check in yet, but they had monopolized the staff's time with their rude demands. "I'll never grant an early check-in again," Amie resolved.

Linda assured her that all early check-ins are not that bad. Then, the phone rang from Room 122, and Amie said, "You get this one. Maybe you can calm them?"

"Thanks a lot," Linda laughed, then picked up the phone.

Amie heard animated talking on the other end.

"Let me see if I heard you correctly," Linda said in a professional voice. "You're concerned that the gentleman in the room next to you *looks* like he might be a snorer, and you are afraid that your family will be disturbed tonight. Is that correct, sir?"

Amie could clearly hear the male voice complaining, even though Linda's phone was several feet from where she stood.

As the man talked, Linda responded with a chorus of "Uh huh," "I see," "I get it," "Mmm," and other concerned phrases. "Mr. Williams, my husband George is a snorer, and I know exactly what you mean.

Sometimes it gets really bad, and you just can't sleep. We don't want you to experience that on your vacation."

The male voice talked again but a little quieter this time.

When the man ran out of steam, she said, "Okay, Mr. Williams, let's not borrow trouble. If you find that there is a snoring problem tonight that interferes with your sleep, call us, and we'll see what we can do about it."

More male talking continued from the man on the other side of the phone.

"Oh yes, snoring can be a terrible problem. Yes….yes…okay, you make sure you call us if the snoring is a problem. Now why don't you go check out Pool Two? It appears to be almost empty at the moment." She paused to listen. "Oh, yes, you can see beautiful sunsets from the path in front of the resort." Another pause. "Yes, and from your patio." Another pause. "Okay, bye now! Enjoy your day."

Linda ended the call by pressing the receiver down onto the phone base with a succinct *click*.

"Okay. I think they will be fine now," Linda said after she hung up.

"Wow! How did you calm him down?" Amie asked in amazement. "He has already had it out with me and staff in at least two other departments. It's absolutely ridiculous!"

"It is all about finding common ground. Once you sympathize with him and take his side, he no longer has any need to yell at you."

"Well, you did a great job, Linda," Amie said with admiration. "By the way, I didn't realize you were married…"

Linda just smiled.

◊ ◊◊◊ ◊

The rest of the day had its own curveballs and problems to be solved.

A happy young couple who came to Chelan for their honeymoon showed up with reservations that the girl's mom had paid for as a wedding gift, and they were eager to check in and enjoy their vacation. However, Amie could not find the reservation in their system. Linda and Amie tried desperately to figure out what went wrong because the reservation was not found under either of their names or their mom's name, and most of the guests who were due to arrive today had already checked in.

Amie called all the other hotels in Chelan to see if the couple was booked in one of those properties instead. Linda finally realized that the reservation that the girl's mom had booked was for today's dates but one year later. Amie and Linda were relieved that they had figured out the issue, but the couple standing in front of them still did not have accommodations, and there were several people in line behind them.

Amie's Aunt Debbie showed up to help, and she and Linda assisted the other people in line while Amie went back to calling all the other properties to see if they had an opening. Each of the properties were busy with their own check-ins, so Amie had to wait on hold for long periods of time with each of them before she could talk to someone. Without fail, every hotel she called was at full capacity. The new husband and wife, who had been troopers throughout this process, were starting to get desperate. The young lady's eyes had filled with unshed tears. Meanwhile, other customers had been checked in and had left for their rooms.

Linda looked at Debbie and said, "Code purple?"

"Code purple," Debbie confirmed. Then, addressing the young couple, she said, "I'll be right back."

Amie looked at Linda quizzically, but Linda just gave her a smile.

A few minutes later, Debbie came back and addressed the young couple: "Take this card to this address about three miles out of town. They have a room that you can book. It is a no-frills property with no amenities–just a room–but it is a lot less expensive than the rooms here." She then handed them another card. "This is a pass for you to use our swimming pools, Jacuzzi tubs, and weight room. Consider it our wedding present to you. And it looks like we will see you next year for your anniversary trip."

The young couple was relieved, and the girl was crying now for real. Debbie went around the counter and gave her a hug and shook the young man's hand. "Have the best honeymoon ever!" Debbie said merrily as the couple left to go to the Cedar Lodge.

Amie looked at her aunt in awe. "What is code purple?" Amie demanded to know.

Aunt Debbie said, "Come to my office, I'll explain."

Debbie sat down at her desk, and Amie sat in the chair across from it, facing her.

"We are part of the local lodging association," Debbie began. "Several years ago, at one of our meetings, we were talking about how awful it is when there is a situation where another room is needed and everyone is booked. That young couple that was here on their honeymoon was a good example because they had made a good faith effort to stay here, but a mistake was made with the dates, and it is now impossible to find them another room here. There are also cases when a pipe breaks and floods the room below it, and we need to place a guest elsewhere. As you know, during high season, we are booked solidly, as is every other hotel, motel, and bed and breakfast around. So, our lodging association came up with a plan. A couple of less expensive hotels volunteer to keep a room or two available and not book it. The rest of the hotels know which hotel has the empty room or rooms and only refer someone there if it is a real hardship case. If none of us sends a referral by 8 o' clock at night, the hotel puts up its vacancy sign, and it is generally able to fill that room for the night."

"Why does the other hotel agree to do that? Why don't they just want to fill the room in advance and make sure it fills and they make money on it?" Amie asked.

"Two reasons," Aunt Debbie explained. "One is simple. We are in the service business, and we all feel

167

badly when we can't accommodate someone, especially when it is someone who really thought they had planned ahead. So, the hotel that leaves a room open is doing their part to help the wayward traveler, so to speak."

"And the other reason?"

"The hotels that leave the rooms open are usually the ones that don't have any amenities, and they can't charge nearly as much on the open market as the full-service hotels can. When they get a last-minute room request, they can offer it a higher rate, closer to our prices, and the customer will pay it because there are no other options. So, the basic hotels can command a higher rate, and we can allow the customer to use our amenities, which is a special perk for the hotel guest."

"So it's a win-win system," Amie said, nodding.

"Yes. We have found that it works really well as long as we are really discerning and only use it occasionally. This couple seemed like they were worth a code purple since they had every intention of being our guest, and their room was pre-paid well in advance, just for the wrong year."

"Why is it called 'code purple'?"

"We wanted to use a code word in case one of the hotels had to make the phone call in front of the guests in question so they wouldn't know what we were talking about. At our hotel association meeting, we talked about using code red or code blue, but those terms already have established meanings. We chose the name 'code purple' because our chairman was wearing purple that day, as were a couple other members. So, the whole idea of 'code purple' has become a system that really works. Keep it on the down low though. Only a couple people are supposed to know about it per hotel."

Amie was pleased to be let in on a closely-guarded secret. She had only one hour left on her shift, and she wondered how much more could happen today.

After coming back to the check-in desk, she found out when a couple of the resorts' guests, the Walkers, entered the lobby. They wanted to do a group reservation for Thanksgiving weekend and thought they would need about 22 rooms. Amie's eyes grew wide when she heard the amount of rooms needed. This was a BIG family.

Amie consulted the reservation grid and saw that they still had many rooms available for the nights in question. Mrs. Walker had everything organized on a spreadsheet that had the names of the guests for each room, the number of guests in each, whether they needed two beds or one, whether they needed a roll-away bed, etc. Amie looked at Linda helplessly. She had never made a reservation of this magnitude and didn't know where to start.

She gave somewhat panicked look to Linda, "Code pink?" and both of them burst out laughing at the timely joke.

She apologized to the guest for laughing and admitted that she had never done a reservation like this before. Linda messaged Debbie to come out.

Debbie came and greeted the guests, asked them a few questions, and asked if it would be okay to work on this over the next few days and give them the proposal before they checked out at the end of the week. The Walkers were okay with waiting because they knew it was a complicated reservation.

It was almost time for Amie to be off work, so Debbie told her that she would train her on large group reservations tomorrow, because today was crazy enough for one day.

Amie went home that day for a greater appreciation of her coworker Linda, her aunt Debbie, and the resort industry as a whole.

CHAPTER FIFTEEN
Hope Handles Things

"Hope, I was wondering if you could hold down the fort for a couple hours?" Uncle Joe asked. "I have a meeting in town."

"Sure! I think we can handle it. There are only a couple new rentals at noon, and four rentals at one o' clock, so we'll be fine."

"Thanks, kiddo! I'll go tell Ron and Pete that it will just be you three for a while," he mentioned as he briskly walked toward the dock area.

Hope watched her Uncle Joe drive off in the direction of town, then consulted the rental log.

One friendly couple who had a noon reservation came at a quarter to twelve, and Hope went through the waivers with them, had them sign the paperwork, and she got them fitted for life jackets before sending them down to the docks. She watched Pete greet them and show them the features of the watercraft they were renting. The docks were too far away for Hope to hear the conversation, but she saw that they were laughing.

171

Hope was lost in thought as she watched the couple mount their jet skis, so she didn't notice three rough-looking males approach the office shack where she was working. They looked to be close to thirty years old each.

"Excuse me, beautiful," the first guy said, stepping close to her. Hope could smell the stench of alcohol on his breath. "We have a reservation for jet skis."

"What's your name?" Hope asked, consulting the list.

"The better question is, what is *your* name?" guy number two returned her question with another question.

"My name is Hope," she countered. Since there was only one remaining reservation for noon, and it was for three jet skis, she knew this must be the one. "Anthony Davis?" she asked evenly.

"That's me, babe," the second guy said as he walked toward her.

Hope was very uncomfortable with the way the guys were looking at talking to her. She looked around to see what resources were available in case she needed help. She wished she had thought of hiding some pepper spray in the office shack for emergencies but she never expected there would be any issues during the daylight hours. She knew there were no actual weapons but maybe there was a heavy tape dispenser or something to throw at them.

"Here is your paperwork," she stated flatly, handing each guy a clipboard. All of them reeked of too much alcohol.

"Hey, babe, maybe you can come out with us? You'd look good sitting on my jet ski with me," guy number one sneered.

"Nuh uh, I saw her first," guy number two slurred. Guy number three also eyed her hungrily. Hope had never felt so threatened in her life. The guys backed her up into the wall of the shack.

Hope was terrified at what might happen next. She also realized that these guys had no business being on the water in their condition, but she was afraid of what would happen if she refused service to them. She thought they might lay hands on her.

Hope breathed a quick prayer, just in case Aunty Nola's God could hear her, even though she still hadn't made a decision whether to follow God herself.

Just then, she had a moment of inspiration. "Guys," she told them, "unfortunately, your rentals aren't available right now. It looks like the people before you haven't returned them yet. How about you go get a drink in the bar over there, and I'll call you when your jet skis arrive?" She pointed to the bar a block away.

"Maybe you can come with us?" guy number three asked her, spewing beer fumes at her.

"Unfortunately, I'm only fifteen," Hope replied.

"Only *fifteen?!*" guy number one yelled. "Let's get out of here!" The guys walked past their gray car and staggered off in the direction of the bar. Hope immediately grabbed the walkie-talkie on the desk and asked Ron to meet her at the shack right away. Ron and Pete both jogged up to the office shack.

"What's up, Hope?" Ron asked. "You look like you've seen a ghost!"

Hope relayed the story of the three men.

"Call the cops! Now!" Pete ordered.

"Are you sure?" Hope asked.

"Yes!" Pete confirmed firmly grabbing the phone and handing it to Hope.

Four police officers arrived almost immediately. Hope was uncomfortable with all the attention. She assumed that they would've just sent one officer to take her report.

"Miss, were you able to get a name?"

Hope consulted the reservation and got one of their names and contact information.

One of the officers called in his information and found that he was wanted for stealing cars.

"That's their car over there!" Hope exclaimed, just remembering that it was still parked in the lot.

"Where are they?" the officers inquired.

"They are at the bar down the street, I think," Hope replied. "I pointed out the bar to them, and they headed in that direction."

Three of the officers took off and apprehended the three men. Soon, a tow truck came to retrieve their car.

A local reporter–who just so happened to be Yvonne Getzen, who Hope had talked to before,–came by to cover the story, and filmed a bit of the car being towed away.

She wanted to interview Hope, but Hope declined.

Pete and Ron gave Yvonne a few sound bites for the

story, and the remaining police officer gave the reporter the details he was able to share.

Uncle Joe showed up around this time and spoke to the police officer. He gave Hope a protective hug.

The officer said her quick thinking helped avoid a bad situation and help lead to the arrest of some auto thieves.

"Great job, young lady," the police officer nodded his approval.

"Hope, take the rest of the day off," Uncle Joe said to his niece. "I'm so sorry I left you here alone."

"I wasn't alone; I had Pete and Ron down at the dock....but I do want to go home," she admitted, still shaken.

The police officer said, "Let me give you a ride," and Hope got in the front of the police car and he dropped her off at The Guesthouse.

◊ ◊◊◊ ◊

Aunty Nola came rushing out when she saw the police car. "Hope, honey, are you okay?"

"She's okay, she is probably just exhausted. She is quite a clever young lady," the officer informed Aunty Nola.

Hope fell into Aunty Nola's arms, finally letting all the fear and stress out in a torrent of tears.

The two of them went inside and Hope told Aunty Nola all about her day and everything that transpired. Aunty Nola listened to every word, feeling every moment as if she had experienced it herself.

"Oh, my poor darling, you were probably so scared," Aunty Nola cooed. "But you did the exact right thing, you know."

"You mean calling the police?"

"Well, that too, but you remembered to pray when your back was, quite literally, up against the wall. I'm certain that is how you had the right words to say to convince them to leave the property and to go have a drink down the street while they waited."

"Maybe it *was* God who gave me that thought."

"Never forget that, Hope. Even if all else fails you, God never will."

"Thank you, Aunty. I think I'll go take a nap now."

Hope went up to bed and had a comfortable nap, feeling safe and loved at The Guesthouse.

CHAPTER SIXTEEN
Peer Counseling

Aunty Nola bustled around the kitchen preparing a delicious homemade dinner for the girls.

She was making special pizza for everyone using her secret recipes for the dough and the sauce. There would be two pies made, and each girl could select the topping combination for a half of one of the pizzas. Emma always wanted the same three toppings: bacon bits, pineapple chunks, and olives. Hope usually wanted hers to be all veggie but sometimes was in the mood for chicken, if there was some leftover in the fridge. Kendi was generally traditional in her choices, with pepperoni sausage, and olives, and Amie liked hers loaded with everything but the kitchen sink.

On nights like these, Aunty Nola just ate a couple slices from whatever was left over from the girls' pizzas because she liked all of them. She also made garlic twists from the same dough and dipping sauce, and sometimes just the twists were enough to fill her up, especially when she knew dessert was coming!

Kendi was going to make custom coffees for each of them, and Emma planned to bring one of her unique ice cream creations for dessert.

Aunty Nola scheduled a couple nights like this each summer so she and her "Guesthouse Girls" could connect. She found that everyone's schedules got so busy that it was hard to all be together at the same time. Scheduling a special stay-at-home night gave them all a chance to unwind a little, help each other with problems, and share each other's successes.

After the girls enjoyed their pizza, Aunty Nola led them in a conversation. She asked them all to say what was on their mind, whether it was a work problem, a relationship dilemma, or something else they wanted to share.

Kendi started and mentioned that she had been feeling a lack of confidence about her job after her big fiasco in the bake shop. She shared that she was a good student, responsible daughter, and basically a perfectionist, so her disaster day at the bake shop really shook her confidence and no matter how many good things happened at work, that terrible day in the kitchen hung over her head. She kept going over what she did wrong and how she could have done better and how she felt that she failed the Brandons when they really needed her because of their family emergency.

"Not to change the subject, but how's Ben's grandpa doing?" Emma asked.

"He's a lot better," Kendi reported.

"Oh, that's a relief," Aunty Nola replied.

"So, have you talked to the Brandons about your 'Disaster Day?'" Amie asked.

"No. I just went to work the next day. One of their regular employees was in charge of baking when I arrived, and I worked in the espresso area. I don't know if they knew about my fiasco or not." Kendi admitted.

"I think you should talk to Mrs. Brandon about it. You might still be feeling a little bit guilty about how your day went, and maybe if you talked to her, you would help clear the air and be able to move on," Hope suggested.

"That's probably a good idea," Amie agreed. "I know how hard it is to admit a mistake, especially when you are so careful to avoid making them, but it's important to do it to help you move on."

"I think I'll follow your advice," Kendi agreed. "It won't be easy, but I don't want to keep feeling yucky all summer."

"Maybe you could pray about it, too," Emma hesitated. "I know I'm new to this, but isn't He always there to help?"

"He absolutely is, dear." Aunty Nola agreed. "Great advice from all of you, girls. How about you, Emma? What would you like to talk about?"

"Well, ever since I interviewed Mr. Femley for my business blog, I've been feeling really depressed about his whole situation. His only son doesn't want anything to do with him and the store, and his daughter Kimmie and his little grandsons are only here temporarily, and he just has the store. Well, he has friends, but no wife.

He doesn't know if either of his kids will ever be willing to take over the store when he retires and that is pretty upsetting for him." Emma frowned.

"Oh, that's so sad! I can't imagine. He spent his whole life making this store so great and he may just have to sell it to a stranger at some point. That really is a bummer," Kendi agreed.

"I never even knew about this," Amie admitted.

"Well, Emma, you are so compassionate to care about Mr. Femley like that," Aunty Nola began. "I wouldn't worry too much about it. These things have a way of working out. The Bible tells us that in Romans 8:28."

"Didn't you say that the store was about 80 years old?" Hope asked.

"Yes, that's what he told me."

"Well, what if you planned a big party for the store and invite Mr. Femley's son and grandsons to come? Then, maybe the grandsons would decide that they would be interested in taking over the store at some point, or at least they could see their grandpa and make him happy." Kendi suggested.

"That's a lovely idea, dear." Aunty Nola said. "What do you think, Emma?"

Emma had brightened considerably at the suggestion. "I would LOVE to plan a party for the store. I'll ask Mr. Femley if we can do it. You all will help me if he says yes, right?"

There was a chorus of four female voices saying yes, as they suggested ideas and activities for the day.

Emma turned to Amie. "What about your issue?"

"Mine isn't as big of deal because it's a long way off, but I'm struggling because I don't know if I want to come back to Chelan after college…kind of like Mr. Femley's son," Amie stated. "I know my family hopes that I'll come back and work for the resort, but I want to do something in fashion, and that usually means going somewhere like New York, Milan, or Paris. I know I'm a long way from having to decide, but I'm a planner and don't know what to do."

"Maybe you can double major in fashion and business in college," Kendi suggested. "That way, you would be covered whichever direction you took."

"And you could learn how to design in college, and then create an exclusive resort wear line that you could license to different resorts with their logos," Emma suggested, ever the young businesswoman. "You could run your clothing and accessories brand AND the resort."

"And you would have your winters fairly free, and you could travel around promoting your fashion brand when business was slower in Chelan," Hope reminded Amie.

"Wow, your friends have your life all planned for you!" Aunty Nola commented.

"Yeah, and she could marry Josh and have three beautiful blonde children," Emma added mischievously.

"I kind of like the sound of that," Amie agreed. "Now that my life is all planned out, let's do the same thing for Hope!"

Hope grinned. "Okay, I guess, just don't plan any kids for me. Actually, I'm doing okay. I'm still a little bit rattled from the incident at work, but other than that, things are going well. I keep having this feeling that something exciting is about to happen, but I don't know what."

"Are you enjoying your time here, or are you homesick?" Emma asked.

"I LOVE it here. I honestly don't miss anything about home except my mom. I feel guilty knowing I have this great job and situation here at The Guesthouse, and her life isn't very fun," Hope revealed sadly.

"Well, if she is able to come for the Fourth of July celebration, we will have to make sure that the two of you spend lots of time together and she has a wonderful weekend," Aunty Nola promised.

"That would be great. I always wish that she would meet an awesome man who would marry her and take care of her so she wouldn't have to work so hard, but I also don't think that we need to have a man to take care of our problems."

"That's right!" the girls all agreed at once.

"Nevertheless, we still like them a lot," Emma giggled. "I see cute boys every day at work, but usually they are with cute girls. I always hope that my Prince Charming is out there somewhere and just hasn't met me yet. But, if he's not, you'll find me someday in my corner office on Wall Street, happily conquering the business world."

"I have no doubt of that, little one. God definitely has a plan for you, Emma, and all you sweet girls," Aunty Nola assured them. "Keep your eyes on Him, and He will continue to guide you on your journey, no matter what twists and turns may occur. I have a feeling the rest of the summer will shape all of your futures," she predicted.

Turns out, she would be absolutely right.

Did you enjoy Summer Entanglements? If so, please consider giving it a positive review on Amazon and Goodreads.

Look for new books by this author coming soon!

If you have other feedback, you can reach us directly through www.mauishorespublishing.com.

Subscribe to our newsletter to receive occasional updates, giveaways, and other perks.

Follow us:

Facebook   @theguesthousegirlsbooks
Instagram: @judyannkoglin_author
           @mauishorespublishing

About the Author

Judy Ann Koglin is a self-described "jill-of-some-trades, master of none." She grew up in the Seattle area, then attended Washington State University in Pullman, where she earned a degree in Business Administration and Marketing. There, she met Wade, and the two of them married and moved to Richland. Since then, she has enjoyed several mini-careers and eventually earned her MBA.

In her teens and twenties, Judy Ann enjoyed several trips to Chelan and found it to be a magical town. She also spent a teenage summer working in a charming beachside area on the Puget Sound, and she draws on both of these experiences to weave coming-of-age stories such as the ones in The Guesthouse Girls series.

In 2017, Judy Ann and Wade fulfilled a long-time dream and moved to the island of Maui. There, they enjoy spending time at the beach, taking long walks at night, and teaching Sunday school at Hope Chapel. Together, they are the proud parents of two boys, Tyler and Tim, and a daughter in-law Lauren.

Upcoming Books in The Guesthouse Girls Series

Midsummer Adventures- Nov 2020

Late Summer Love - Dec 2020

Upcoming Books in The Autumn Collection

The Autumn of Kendi - Jan 2021

The Autumn of Hope - Feb 2021

The Autumn of Emma - March 2021

The Autumn of Amie - April 2021

Each of these books can be pre-ordered, as they are released, through Maui Shores Publishing.
www.mauishorespublishing.com.

Made in the USA
Las Vegas, NV
01 September 2021